THE VIGILANTE'S LOVER

VOL. 4

Annie Winters
Tony West

www.anniewinters.com
www.tonywestwrites.com

casey shay press

Casey Shay Press
PO Box 160116
Austin, TX 78716
www.caseyshaypress.com

ISBN: 9781938150432

Also available in digital format.
eISBN: 9781938150449

Library of Congress Control Number: 2015934736

FIRST EDITION

Also by Annie Winters

Writing as JJ Knight
The UNCAGED LOVE Series
The FIGHT FOR HER Series

Writing as Deanna Roy
Forever Innocent
Forever Loved
Forever Sheltered

Learn about appearances and events at
www.deannaroy.com

For Annie's Vigilantes

You made this writing journey so fun.

1

JAX

I'm not sure which I'm more pissed about, getting dragged away from Mia, or this punk driving my car.

I don't know any of the Vigilantes who collected me from the hotel in Nashville. They're all southern born and trained, but they must have come through the program after I did.

I am, however, very familiar with the silo we're heading toward. It's under the jurisdiction of Alan Carter, who runs the Missouri silo that Mia and I visited last week. He isn't likely to be at this one, though. The Tennessee silo is a single-missile launcher and primarily serves as a first-stop mission control for Phase One Trainees who have just gotten their first Vigilante orders.

It's where I got mine.

The Aston Martin roars along the highway at high speed. This guy must be at least a Phase Five Driver. He's good. We weave through morning rush hour in Nashville like it isn't even there.

The girl is in the front passenger seat. The other guy who came to the hotel is driving another car, but we've left him far behind. He's not a pro driver like this sleazebag.

He keeps trying to put his hand on the girl's knee, and she keeps finding ways to knock it off without causing a fuss. I want to break his hands, which is allowed in the Vigilante code. We can reprimand other Vigilantes. Even fight them. Just no murder.

Other than me, of course. I'm under a kill order. Fair game.

"So why aren't you following Standard Execution Protocol on this?" I ask. On a typical preordered kill, you use a snuff dart and drive the body to the closest crematorium on the Vigilante books. They dispose of the body in a way that nobody ever finds it.

That's why most funeral homes are so swank. They get a pretty penny for taking care of this bit of dirty work for us.

We've got two facilities in Nashville, and yet we're driving away from the city. They must have some other plan for me first.

The girl turns around in her seat, knocking the asshole's hand off her leg for the hundredth time. "Just following orders," she says.

Sutherland's, I assume. I wonder if Jovana has already made it to Washington. Damn it.

I'm restrained by a device I've never seen before. It's some sort of electromagnetic handcuff. Sam would hate it. It's inelegant, bulky, and probably requires more power than necessary.

The restraint consists of two metal circles that are magnetically sealed. Between the heavy cuffs is a silver power box. The whole gizmo probably weighs ten pounds.

"Can't you send someone for my suitcase?" I ask. "Some Phase One?" I frown at my pajama pants and the T-shirt I was handed.

"You aren't going to need your suitcase," the

driver jerk says. "Everything burns in the end."

I sit back against the cushion. So they're going to take me to a crematorium at some point. I still have to wonder what is so threatening about me that they would need to snuff me. Makes no sense. My killing another Vigilante was a violation of the code, and punishment was coming my way. But it wasn't a hanging offense. Not in our world, where collateral damage is part of the job.

I'm not sure I'll live long enough to know why I was dangerous to Sutherland. Mia probably won't ever know of my fate.

I picture her coming out of the bathroom, all fresh and ready for our trip to Washington, and discovering I'm gone. I don't think she'll panic. Hopefully she spotted the ring and got the message from the thief knot. Even though there isn't anything she can do to stop what is happening to me, at least she'll know I didn't desert her.

Since I'm stuck for the foreseeable drive, I decide to take the dead man's path for a moment and think about her. Nothing else in my life deserves my last thoughts.

She's been different from the first moment I saw her, sleeping in that pristine white nightgown, tucked into a bedroom that looked like it still housed her high school memorabilia.

Now that I'm admitting things to myself, I know she caught my interest from the start. I wanted to push her, see where she would bend, how much it took to break her to my will, my needs.

In the end, she broke me.

The sky is blue and calm. The driver weaves around cars as traffic thins out. I picture the red ropes on Mia's bare skin, how she shivered in the moonlight in that field when I stripped her. I almost laugh to remember how she called me out on shredding her nightgown when I had a scanning wand.

She was right. I didn't have to take everything off. I could have detected a recording device without laying a hand on her.

But I hadn't. And I learned how sharply her mind turned, even under extreme duress. Now that I know how innocent she was, she handled that night with unbelievable poise. I was abominable at the hotel, staring at her like a lecherous beast. The image of her pale luminous body in that room is etched into my memory.

I shift uncomfortably on the seat. I'm not

willing to say I've given up the fight on this. Of course I haven't. But an execution in a Vigilante silo isn't something I could imagine anyone escaping. I for damn sure wouldn't have allowed it to happen under my jurisdiction.

I've cut off contact with Sam and Colette for their safety. Good move, truly. If I'm a dead man, I don't need to drag them with me. Hopefully they will think to help out Mia. She has nothing now, not even a home. At least there is that neighbor woman.

We exit to a smaller highway and begin a winding path through the piney woods. I remember this road well from my first Vigilante days. I was an unusual age, starting the program young, the summer I turned twelve. So I was just thirteen when I arrived at this silo for my first mission.

At the time, my father held a director position, running the Miami syndicate. Even so, he was waiting at this silo with my orders.

It was a simple job, the sort of thing they asked young Phase Ones to do. I was to infiltrate a gang of petty thieves who were eluding the local law enforcement. Normally we'd stay out of small-time stuff like this, but one of them had been stalking a thirteen-year-old girl, and they wanted me to get the boy to make a big enough mistake that he'd be carted off to juvie and out of range of this girl.

The boys were planning a minor haul at a garage in a suburb of Memphis. They didn't know it was also a meth lab.

I hooked up with them by staking out the same garage and acting like it was my turf. This went the predictable way. I had to fight one of their guys, and when I beat him inside six seconds, a knife pressed to his throat, they agreed we could do this job together.

The mission went perfectly. The bulk of the boys made off with the tools and spare parts they were going for, but I showed the target boy the bigger haul, the meth. I didn't have to do a thing after that. He returned to the lab on his own and was nabbed by the cops in a sting on the whole operation, one we knew was coming.

That girl would be in her mid-thirties by now. I hope she's lived a calm and happy life due to our intervention.

The entrance of this silo is smaller than the Missouri one, just a metal door. As a Vigilante assigned to it, I would enter by one of the hatches out in the field, going down a long ladder to the tunnel that led to the control room and the silo itself.

But since I'm a prisoner who must be led in, we take the door instead of a hatch. The driver drops us off, and the woman leads me up to the rusting facade. All the openings to silos look abandoned. This one is particularly convincing, covered in graffiti and laced with vines.

"Is that asshole always your driver?" I ask her.

"Unfortunately," she says.

"Perfectly legal to break his fingers," I say.

She almost cracks a smile as we approach the silo entrance.

The iron gate swings open, revealing a set of bright steel doors. Two Vigilante guards wait inside. There is no glass data hall like in most silos, but nobody needs any information as we enter. They all know a dead man walking when they see him.

I'm surprised to see Alan Carter himself as we pass through a series of security checks.

"Slumming it?" I ask him. "Didn't want to miss the festivities?"

His face is poker straight. "Executing a Vigilante is serious business," he says. "I'm doing everything by the book."

"Really?" I ask. "I wasn't given a snuff dart on sight. That's by the book."

"You were in the presence of a special," Carter says. "She bought you a little time."

I'm not sure if I'm supposed to be grateful.

"Now that we're off protocol, what's it going to be?" I ask him. "Poison? Old-fashioned bullet? Something new and exciting?" My voice is deadpan.

"Take him to interrogation," Carter says.

That's an odd choice for completing a kill order. When I raise an eyebrow, Carter adds, "We don't have an execution room."

Few silos do. When that sort of mission is called for, it usually happens off site.

When we enter the small room, I recognize the white walls and table, the black dome recording our every word and movement.

And Paulson.

That damn Vigilante is everywhere. He's probably not too happy I stole his car in New Mexico.

Or that I've creamed his face both times we've met.

I'm only two steps in the room when he leaps forward and takes a potshot, his fist slamming into my jaw. My hands are still locked into the magnetic cuffs, so I just accept the blow without flinching.

"You're destroying my pretty face for the casket," I say.

In response, his elbow connects with my belly.

I bend over from the impact but don't make a sound. When I straighten, I say, "I see you're a much better fighter when the other guy is restrained."

He clocks me one more time on the chin. I spin with it to avoid a concussion. The woman who led me into the room steps back and the door closes between us. Carter stands in the corner, watching.

"One more," he tells Paulson.

While Paulson seems to ponder his next strike, Carter takes a skeleton key like the one I used to escape his silo and sticks it to the face of the table. He punches a button right as Paulson slams his knee into my gut.

With a sizzle and a spark, the electronics in the room go out. Carter tosses his own jacket over the dome. "That was a nice trick you pulled back in Missouri," he says to me. "And the perfect scenario for what we're about to do."

I wonder darkly if they are going to torture

me, something not ordinarily sanctioned by Vigilantes.

But he says to Paulson, "That's enough. You can go."

Paulson scowls but walks up to the scanner to pass through the door.

I shake off the blows. I'm apparently going to live to see another five minutes. And with the tech down in the room, we can talk freely.

"He could use another round of fight training," I tell Carter.

"You're exceptionally tough," Carter says. "He works well enough for regular humans." He motions to a chair. "Sit, before I have to explain to someone upstairs why my tech team is so slow at restoring the eyes and ears of the Vigilante network to this room."

I drop into a chair. I have no idea what to expect now.

2

Mia

Obviously Jax's ex-lover isn't going to underestimate me this time.

I wake up from what I assume was some drug, unable to move. The city flies by. We're still in the blue Acura, and Jovana is driving.

She has me tied with six different ropes and at least ten knots. I recognize all the ones that I can see, but I have no hope of escaping from them. My fingers are literally tied down, then my wrists, then the ropes crisscross all over the place, lashing me to the seat.

"You're awake," she says, her "w" more like a "v." The accent is strong. It makes her seem more exotic and sexy. Her black hair is shiny and sleek, tied up in a loose French twist. Her cheekbones are straight from a magazine, and the black dress she's wearing looks like it just strutted down a runway.

Jealousy spikes through me. So this is the woman who was Jax's undoing.

Jovana drives the Acura like a demon from hell, cornering the curves so hard that my head, the only free part of my body, snaps from side to side.

"Stupid civilian vehicle," she says, then lapses into a stream of what I assume is Russian.

"You don't have a fancy Vigilante car?" I ask, then lean my head away at her withering glare.

"Shut up," she says. "It's bad enough I have to endure your presence. I don't want to hear your yapping mouth."

All jealousy evaporates. Jax chose a real peach. Maybe she's mad that I'm not quaking in my ankle boots.

I look down at my trussed-up body. I swear I'm tied up more often than I'm loose these days. What a crazy life.

I don't care a whit that she just told me to shut

up. If I offend or annoy her, all the better. "Where are we going?" I ask. I shake my head, trying to clear the fuzziness, probably left over from whatever she gave me to make it easier to tie me up. I guess I should be glad it wasn't a snuff dart.

She ignores me, punching her finger on the screen. When she finds nothing but the original owner's data, she taps her phone against it like Colt did. Then she hits a name I'm very familiar with.

Klaus.

I can't picture him clearly, having only encountered him in the dark, his cigarette a small glow of light. But Jax did show me his picture as we prepared to encounter them after the MMA fight. The screen gives nothing away, though, as it links through. Only his name is visible.

The number rings and rings, but does not answer or go to voice mail. Jovana's eyes narrow and she mutters more Russian.

"Not answering your calls? Men are crappy like that," I say.

"Shut up or I'll cut your face," she snaps.

Whoa-kay. I press my lips together. I'll just have to gather information by observing. I look out the windows. We're out of the piney woods. The sun is still in the east and rising. So I wasn't out long and we're driving northeast. I almost ask if we're headed to Washington to meet Sutherland, but then I remember she wants to cut my face.

We can't make it in time for the evening meeting by car. It must be ten hours at normal speeds. Maybe we're heading for an airport. Of course, she can't really risk that with a captive. Jax might have been able to sneak a tied-up girl into the back of a hotel, but they won't ignore me trying to board a plane.

Jovana stabs at the screen again. This time it's a name I don't know. Kovitch.

"What is the nature of this call?" A dark-haired man scowls from the screen, then relaxes. "Jovana? Why are you calling unencrypted on this channel?"

"I've run into a snag," she says. She glances over at me and starts speaking in Russian. Despite not knowing a word of it, I pick out a few names. Sutherland. De Luca. Klaus. And some cities. Knoxville. Washington.

So we're still going that way. I've told Jax about Jovana's meeting, so if he's able to get out of whatever jam he's in, maybe we'll meet up. My heart soars at the thought that we can continue to fight this thing, maybe win it. Clear his name. Get this woman and that Klaus guy—wherever he is now—off our backs.

I try to think about what I'll do if I'm faced with having to kill someone. Can I do it?

Jovana disconnects the call and turns to glare at me. "I can't wait to cut that smirk right off your beastly face," she says.

Yeah, I could kill her.

"Sutherland blowing you off too?" I ask, then wonder why I'm antagonizing her, as her fist connects with my chin. The blow hurts more than it should, and I realize I must be bruised. She hit me some other time. Maybe when I was drugged.

I'm dying to look at my face, but I'm tied up. And afraid of what I look like. I close my eyes and try to feel any injuries. My jaw is aching and there is something strange about my cheek when I smile. Like there's dried blood.

So I shut up. No use getting any more scars than I may already have. I assess the rest of my body, but I can't get any sense of other injuries with the ropes biting into me in so many places.

She tries calling Klaus again and I hold back a

nasty remark. So her partner in crime has cut her off. Jax didn't kill him, I know that. Maybe he's just gone off grid. He did it to Jax before. That's what started this whole thing, at least my part of it.

Jax. I calm myself by picturing his rugged face, that thick dark hair, his gray stormy eyes. I've known I was in love with him for a while now, but Jax isn't the sort of guy you hand your heart over to. It's likely to get shot right out of your hands.

But I can nurse that feeling anyway. It's new to me, tender and exhilarating at the same time. He can't be in too much duress if he was able to tie that thief knot. But they were quiet. I was in the very next room and didn't hear a thing when whoever took him arrived.

The car dings that it is low on fuel. Jovana curses. I'm sure she'd rather have a Vigilante car, and I wonder why she can't get one. But if Klaus is blowing her off, she might be in trouble with the Vigilantes. Maybe that's why she came for me. Her last conversation with Sutherland didn't go well either, the one I overheard in the parking lot. She accused him of avoiding her.

Something is definitely up. Maybe that's why she needs me. Some sort of leverage. A hostage. I don't know. The only person who might care about me is Jax.

I assume he does.

Of course he does.

He brought me along. He teased me with that gun to get me past that fear. My blood rushes just thinking about it. I believe with all my heart that he intends to keep me with him.

I have to hold on to that right now.

We pass a gas station, and I glance over at the fuel gauge. It says we can only go thirty more miles. The road is well traveled, so there will be more stations, but I wonder how she's going to hide a bound woman from anyone who might pull up to a pump next to her. In broad daylight, that's going to get some attention. Unlike Vigilante cars, which have special windows to hide the interior, anyone can see right in.

As the number continues to drop with Jovana's lead-foot driving, I start to form a plan.

3

JAX

Carter leans forward on the interrogation table. He seems tired.

"Jax," he says, "after you left my silo, I did some digging." He runs his fingers through his short-cropped graying hair. "There are a lot of abnormalities in the data, starting about eighteen months ago."

I sit down in the chair opposite him, careful not to bump the jacket covering the video mechanism.

"What did you find?" I ask. I know how high

this goes, but I'm curious if Carter does. Probably so, if he felt the need to knock out the power to the room to avoid Vigilante higher-ups from listening in.

"I know that Klaus isn't dead. I know he's working with Sutherland and a special." He rubs his thumbs against his eyebrows. "And I know they are recruiting people for something big, something technology driven."

"What sort of thing?" I ask. This last part is new.

"Sutherland is gathering Phase Tens and taking them off grid." He lifts his Identipad as if to show me, then thinks better of it and sets it down again. "Better not tip them off that I'm working in here," he says.

"Who?" I ask.

"Gabriella Soto from Mexico, a poison specialist. She allegedly died in a shootout four months ago. Jason Ferro from Detroit, a technology guy, like Klaus. His death record was cleaned a little better, so I'm not sure what his cause was."

"How do you know they're involved?" I ask.

"Their cars." He grins. "When a Vigilante car is transferred to a new owner, there's a record. Their cars seem to be driven by ghosts."

"Nice," I say. "So what do you think this team is for?"

"I was hoping you would know," he says.

The lights flicker overhead. "We're out of time," he says. "I'm going to fake your death just like they've been doing, and get you to that car you stole from Paulson. Stand up for me."

I rise from the chair. "Where am I going?"

"To Washington. To Sutherland. A couple ghost cars were headed that direction. So will you." He claps me on the shoulder. "I'm going to be watching you. You'll have an ID assigned to you, one I've set aside for a while for a Vigilante who disappeared in the Sahara but that I've kept active."

I nod.

"As the power comes up, I'm going to knock you out. When you come to, you'll be in the car with the new ID. I can't guarantee you'll be able to stay off grid. But I can get you started, and I'll send people to help you as I can."

He turns grimly to the jacket covering the dome. "The whole network is at risk now. Nobody can trust anybody, with things going on like they are."

"I'll get to the bottom of it. I'm a dead man anyway," I tell him.

He yanks the jacket off the dome. "Power's back. Now that we can document things, it's time to go off grid for good." He clicks an invisible button on the table. A panel slides open, and he lifts a silver case from a hidden compartment.

"You going to fight or can I do this with just us?" he asks.

"I don't need an audience," I say bitterly.

He pulls the syringe out, a yellow one for the snuff dart. My eyes follow Carter's hand as he moves toward me.

"I'd ask for last words, but I don't really give a shit," Carter says.

"Do what you've got to do," I say.

He pricks my arm. I've seen a snuff dart used a dozen times, and I've administered them myself. I know what it looks like to go down with one. It's clean and easy, a crumple to the ground.

I plan to emulate that look so that the dart is convincing, but then I realize it's happening without my trying.

Suddenly I wonder if this was all a double cross, a ploy to make me an easy mark. They kept me from putting up a fight.

The room starts to swirl, and I lose feeling in my legs. My knees hit the ground in a bruising crash.

My body starts to fall forward. I think my head is going to bash the floor but mercifully, before that can happen, everything goes black.

4

MIA

We pass six more gas stations, and I can feel Jovana's concern growing. Maybe there's too many people at them. Maybe she's forgotten civilian cars aren't always electric like Vigilante ones.

I'm not going to clue her in.

I'm bound in so many ways, I can't get loose. But I'm not gagged. I can scream.

I can also kick at the dash. If Jovana gets out to pump gas, I'm pretty sure I can do some serious damage to this car while she's outside. Maybe I can set off an alarm or even break the gearshift and make the car inoperable.

I have to try.

The gauge says five miles to empty. We're on the outskirts of Knoxville. Maybe we're heading somewhere within the range of the gas she has. I feel weary, unable to move in all the restraints, the ropes rubbing my upper arms even through the jacket.

We approach a station and this time Jovana slows down. My heart speeds up. We're going to stop.

I try to avoid staring at her or looking anxious. I keep my eyes cast down on my lap. Still, I watch her from my peripheral vision.

She pulls up to the farthest pump so that I'm on the outside. Unless someone walks by, no one will notice me. Even so, before she gets out, she reaches into the backseat and snatches up the tarp that was on the car before we stole it.

And she covers me, head to toe.

I sneeze from the stirred-up dust. I can't see anything now other than the glow of light through the fabric. Crap.

I hear her door open, then close. I listen carefully for the sound of the gas nozzle going into the tank. She's outside and not paying attention to me.

I have to go for it.

I twist and lift my legs, trying to maneuver toward the center of the car. My feet swing up and I kick at the dash, hearing a satisfying crunch that might be the screen.

The ball that controls the dash is in the console, and I keep kicking, hoping I can break it off. My feet find the steering wheel, but that seems futile. At this awkward angle, I can't get enough power in my legs to do anything to it.

But my foot does find the windshield-wiper lever and I kick until I hear it break off.

The door swings open.

"What the hell are you doing?" Jovana asks. Something closes around my ankle. I guess she's trying to hold me.

I kick with all my might, pummeling my feet at her.

"You little bitch!" she says and lets go.

I think she's retreated because I don't connect with her anymore.

The door slams.

I'm alone in the car again. I jerk hard at the

ropes, trying to get all the wiggle room I can muster to give me leverage to kick at the controls again. I hear another crunch.

Then I feel air.

My car door is open.

I still can't see, but then the world is brighter as the tarp moves.

Maybe she'll drag me out of the car and leave me here. I just have to be more trouble than I'm worth.

I jerk against the bonds, trying to free an elbow enough that I can get a shot at her.

Jovana grabs me. It's not hard to keep me still since I'm mostly tied down anyway.

I feel a prick in my arm and something cold runs into my veins. I look down and see a needle withdrawing from my sleeve. She's stabbed me blindly.

But the drug moves through me. My stomach turns, and I feel sick.

I wonder if it's the same thing that drugged me before, or one of the Vigilante poisons. Will I wake up in a few hours, or do I have seven minutes until I'm dead?

My head feels heavy, too much for my neck to

hold. It lolls to one side like I'm not in control.

Jax would be so disappointed in me. Despite my best efforts, I'm failing at everything. Caught by the enemy. Unable to get loose from the ropes despite all my practice. Drugged.

I won't cry. I won't. Vigilantes don't cry.

But my eyes burn. I'm bitter and angry at myself for not being more careful, for not realizing Jovana would track her Vigilante watch, for getting caught in the first place.

I don't deserve to be part of their network. As a spy, I'm a total failure. I have no training. I mess up the basics.

The color starts to drain out of the light I can see. I sense Jovana getting back in the car and starting the engine.

By the time the car lurches forward, I'm falling into darkness.

5

JAX

Wherever I am, it's pitch black.

My head vibrates with a rumbling under the floor. I jostle a little in the tight confines. The air is hot and smells of rubber and dust.

But I'm not dead. So Carter was playing it straight back at the silo. The yellow dart that he gave me wasn't a snuff poison. Just a drug.

The heavy magnetic cuffs are off my wrists. I shift my ankles. I'm not restrained in any way. That's a good sign. But I'm heavy, like I'm still sedated. Half-conscious.

I feel suspicious. If they trusted me, I shouldn't need to be drugged. Or locked up in the dark.

I breathe hard and fast for several seconds, infusing my brain with oxygen as I run my hands along the bottom of the space. Metal. Carpet. A rounded form bumped out on both sides. For tires. I'm in the trunk of a car.

A red light starts blinking, slow and steady. Probably a motion detector that lets them know I'm awake. I wonder if they are listening.

"Who's driving?" I ask.

No answer. I guess not.

But the car slows down. They've noticed the alarm.

Just in case my situation isn't what it seems, I feel around for something I can use as a weapon. Tire jack. Suitcase. Anything. But it's just me in the trunk. Still in my pajama pants and the T-shirt from the hotel when I left Mia.

Mia. I wonder where she is. I have no idea how much time has passed.

All Vigilante car trunks have a false bottom. My fingers find the edges of the covering, and I flip the lever hidden underneath. The trapdoor lifts an inch as we roll to a stop.

I scoot as far as I can away from the opening so I can lift it enough to reach inside. There might be a cache of weapons or something else I can use.

But the door isn't made to open while someone's sitting on it.

I'm out of time anyway, as the latch clicks on the trunk lid. I spin onto my back, feet out, ready to fight. I force my adrenaline to surge to combat the downward pull of the drug.

The sky appears in degrees, and the body of a man in running gear.

Seriously?

It's Paulson. He grins at me like a big ape. "Happy to see me?" he says.

I resist the urge to knock him backward. He holds out a hand as if he's going to assist, but I push off with my arms, neatly hopping out of the trunk.

"Nice dismount," he says wryly. "I told them the drugs weren't going to be enough for you. Too bad that shiner messes up your youthful good looks."

I touch my hands to my face. The side of one eye is swollen. "Easy shot at a restrained man," I say and take a look around.

He shrugs. "All for show."

No mention of how I bested him at the silo as well as in the car chase. Sore points, probably.

We're near an old covered wooden bridge. A river trickles below. The road is narrow. The air is a little cooler than in Nashville, and the trees are less piney, more deciduous. They're showing fall colors. "We've gone farther east," I say.

"Yeah, we're in Virginia," he says. "That dart knocked you out for hours."

"We're traveling fast," I say.

Paulson closes the trunk and pats the bumper of the car. "Yeah, nice to have my car back."

He's right. It is his. The one I stole from him and stashed in Tennessee, when I met up with Mia and got my Aston Martin back.

"Why was I in the trunk?" I ask.

"Dead man don't ride in the seats," he says.

Right again. I forgot they faked my death.

"Where are we headed?" I ask.

"D.C. We should make it in about two hours," he says.

"How'd you find your car?" I ask. "I left it cloaked in a seriously remote town."

Paulson jerks his thumb at the front. "Your

friend has been in contact with Carter for a few days now. He asked for cover yesterday when he got blown. Apparently that special of yours called him when you got up close and personal with that prosthetic-skin kill device. He had to bow out as a Vigilante or face a tribunal for helping you."

"Sam is here?"

"That's what I'm saying." Paulson thumps on the back window.

The passenger door opens and a dark buzzed head appears. Sam turns, speaking into a Blackphone, and waves. He holds up a finger, telling us to wait a second.

"He's up," Sam says into the receiver. "I'll fill him in." He shuts off the phone and stares at it with admiration. "Damn, I do good work. I can talk like I'm not on the run with a dead man."

"Hey, Sam," I say. "Figured I'd meet you in hell."

He strides up to me and smacks my back. "You've got a death wish lately, boy."

"Funny what happens when you're under a kill order."

He hands me a Vigilante watch. "Your fake ID. Answer to Jed Buchanan."

I strap it on. "You don't happen to have any clothes for me somewhere, do you?"

Paulson grunts in annoyance. "You and your fancy pants."

Sam shakes his head. "We'll stop somewhere before we hit headquarters." He glances down at my pajama bottoms. "Based on the, um, situation, seems like this is better than what it could have been."

"Pink bondage rope," Paulson says.

Sam stifles a laugh.

No telling how much they watched or recorded. Mia would be mortified. I have no desire to know what they saw.

"Fine," I say. "What sort of intel do we have on the situation?"

"Let's get back on the road," Sam says. "We can update you en route."

"He's a lousy driver," I say. "Let me take the wheel."

Paulson snorts. "You're coming off the juice dart. No way are you taking over my car." He heads back to the driver's side door.

"Chill, Jax," Sam says. "They dosed you hard so you'd pass for dead. Had to bring your respiration down to untrackable levels. You're bound to feel like shit."

"I feel fine." It's a lie. I can still feel the slowness of my responses. But I can fake it.

"Get in the back," Sam says. "I'll let you know where we are with this."

I open the door and sink into the leather, angry that Paulson is along for the ride. I want to ask about Mia, if she's been picked up. But not around him. Someone should probably know who she is, that she's the descendant of Vigilante One. More than just a special. The granddaddy of specials. But I say nothing.

Sam gets in beside me, and Paulson drops the car into high-speed auto-drive. The scenery whips past.

I sit back. "So, anybody figure out why Sutherland's recruiting Vigilantes and faking their deaths?"

"No idea," Sam says. "But there's a lot of them, all foreign recruited."

"Anybody tracking where they go?" I ask.

"We've got a watch on their cars. A few have headed toward D.C., but most go inactive after a couple days." Sam passes me an Identipad.

"Is this safe to use?" I ask.

Sam nods. "It's Paulson's. We had to bring him along since I'm deactivated."

"Why this bozo?" I ask, not lowering my voice. Paulson should know I don't trust him.

"He's got a vendetta against you, which makes him perfect for throwing off suspicion that he's helping. He was also part of your death, and we want as few people as possible to know you're still around."

Right on all counts. Still, I wish Carter had brought in some other Vigilante. Any other Vigilante.

Sam taps the pad to bring up the screen. "Now if I had to guess, either these supposedly dead Vigilantes are together somewhere, or they've all gone on missions."

"No telling what Sutherland is using them for, but if it's anything like with Klaus, it isn't good," I say. "How the hell are we supposed to find invisible, off-grid, supposedly dead Vigilantes?"

"We're looking for slipups," Sam says. "And we might have found one in Germany." He swipes at the screen. "A Vigilante killing. By another Vigilante."

I narrow my eyes. "Where's Jovana?" The last time a Vigilante died by Vigilante hands, she was there. And convincing me to make the kill.

I want to strangle her.

Sam swipes at his forehead. "Jovana's off grid."

"But I saw her in Nashville."

"She's a special. Specials aren't tracked."

"Did they find Klaus after I dropped him at the fight?"

Sam turns to me. "He was there?"

"He was the one who poisoned me. Mia didn't tell you?"

Sam rubs his eyes. "She was a little panicked trying to get you an antidote."

"So Klaus is still out there."

"You didn't kill him?"

I shake my head. "Too much Vigilante blood on my hands already."

"You're creating enemies," Sam says.

"They can wait in line."

Paulson turns around to us. "We've got a network-wide bulletin coming up," he says. "You probably want to see this."

We lean forward to look at his dash screen.

Sutherland comes on. He looks concerned, his gray hair neatly combed, a military-style jacket on. He's trying to convey authority, right down to the strategy map behind him.

He clears his throat. "Earlier today, a German Vigilante by the name of Mars Bronson killed one of his fellow countrymen." Sutherland's face is grim. "And just an hour ago, two more Vigilante executions within the network were reported in Russia and China."

He walks to the strategy map. "We have reports of blackouts here and here." He taps North Korea and Afghanistan, then turns to face the camera with a somber expression. "We have some sort of uprising within the network."

He walks back to a chair. The camera zooms in on his face.

"This feels rigged," I say to Sam.

He nods. "Agreed."

Sutherland goes on. "But we have a solution. After one of our own operatives went rogue last year, we were able to implement correctional initiatives to stem the damage."

Sam elbows me. "You required correctional initiatives."

Paulson grunts. "Still does."

Sutherland continues, "We are sending our finest minds to these other networks to share our strategies so that we can uphold the integrity and safety of humanity."

"That's a lot of ten-dollar words," Sam mutters.

I sit back. "He has no intention of sharing strategies," I say.

Paulson turns around. "What's he up to, then?"

I look out the window at the trees blowing past. "This is a takeover."

6

Mia

I'm alive.

My awareness comes back in stages. The car stopping. A door slamming. Footsteps. Voices. I try to open my eyes. Light barely makes it through the fabric. I'm still covered by the tarp.

Still bound to the seat of the Acura.

My door opens and the tarp comes off. The brightness is so intense that my skull feels like it might explode. I just want to go back to sleep.

"She's a beauty," a male voice says.

"She's drugged. Do whatever you want with

her," Jovana snaps.

This jolts me fully awake. I squint and look at the man staring at me. He has short curly hair and merry eyes. "I think she's up," he says. His smile tells me he has no intention of doing anything Jovana says.

"You want me to untie her?" he asks.

"Be careful," Jovana says. "Look what she did to the car."

The man looks past me at the damage I inflicted to the dash. "Too bad. These are nice vehicles. For civilians, anyway."

"This car is toast due to the little wretch." Jovana has her hip stuck out, standing behind the man.

"I don't think she's going to fight me as we move to the other car." He meets my eyes. "Are you now, love?"

His endearment makes Jovana press her lips together in displeasure.

I look him over. White button-down shirt, rolled up at the cuffs. Khakis. He has a laid-back air that doesn't fit any of the Vigilantes I've met so far. But he's wearing their signature watch. He must be one.

"I'll be fine," I manage to squeak out. My throat is raw. I'm terribly thirsty. I wonder what harm all these drugs might be doing to me. I have to get away from Jovana.

Or take her out somehow.

"I'm Mark," the man says. "Part of the network. Friend of Jovana."

I want to tell him that he's no friend of mine, then, but his merry eyes keep me silent. I guess even evil bitches can have nice friends.

Or maybe he's putting on a big show. I seem to remember Jax talking about mood-enhanced speech, early on, when he still thought I was the enemy.

God, how much things have changed in the week since I met him.

How much I've changed.

But I know such a training exists. So I'm wary.

"I'm going to untie you," Mark says. "So we can move you to a new car. You're not going to fight us, are you?"

Jovana shoves her head over his shoulder. "I hope you do, because then I'll stick you with another dart," she says.

Ugh. I want to punch her. I look away and stare at Mark. "I'll be good," I say.

"Excellent," he says. He looks over the ropes. "Geez, Jovana, did you use every knot in the book?"

"No," I say. "She stuck to grade-school versions. A mix of binding knots and a few pointless splicers. The only thing they have going for them is that there are so many."

Mark raises his eyebrows and cracks a wide smile. "She's a wily one, Jove," he says over his shoulder.

"So she knows a few knots," Jovana says. "Isn't going to help her if I snuff-dart her."

Mark starts plucking at the knots. "Did you see the update on Jax?" he asks her.

"I've been in a civilian car," Jovana says. "I don't know anything."

"He got snuffed. Tennessee silo, about two hours ago."

A searing pain bolts through me. What do they mean by snuffed? Dead?

"Good," Jovana says. "About time they caught him." She sneers at me. "I'm sure this one calling into the network on an open line is what did him in. Did you know she left my own watch in her car?

Like tracking a teenager on Snapchat, it was. Took less than ninety seconds to find her."

I'm still trying to understand what has happened. "Are you saying Jax is dead?" My voice betrays me, warbling and unsteady.

Mark gives up on untying the knots and flicks his wrist, dropping a knife from a holster. He cuts through the first set. "Yes, love. Alan Carter administered the dart himself. They broadcast the video of him going down."

My stomach drops. It can't be true. Jax can get out of any situation, anywhere. He isn't dead. I won't believe it.

I want to throw up. My belly heaves. I don't even care if Mark cuts me loose or not. This is my fault. I called Sam. They found us because of me.

"Don't fret, love," Mark says. "He wasn't a very good man."

I want to hit him. "Yes, he was."

"Oh, look, the girl has fallen in love with the master of women," Jovana says. She leans over Mark again. "Let me give you a clue, girl. Jax didn't care about anybody. A woman was an object he could dress up in Armond's lavish creations to be more entertaining when he poked her hole."

Tears blur my eyes, but I will them away. I don't answer her. Obviously anything she says is tainted by whatever went down last year.

But this is my time to get information out of her. If I do anything in these last days, it will be exonerating Jax. And I no longer care at all if I die doing it. I have nothing left to lose.

Buck up, baby. Don't think about Jax. Just do your job.

"So why did you spend so much time with him, then?" I ask her.

Mark pulls the last rope from my arm, and I rub my skin where it is marked and bruised. I revel in the pain. It will keep me sharp. I want this evil woman to pay, and for Jax to be remembered for the Vigilante he was before her.

"All part of the plan, Mia dear. All part of the plan." Jovana lets out a sardonic laugh.

Mark holds out a hand to me. I refuse to take it.

"I want to see the video," I say.

"Ho ho! She wants to see Jax die," Jovana says. "Maybe she's not the ninny that I thought!"

"She doesn't believe it," Mark says softly. "She needs to see it with her own eyes."

His kindness makes me tear up again. He extends his hand once more, and this time I take it.

"I'm down with watching that," Jovana says. "Let's get to the car so we can get to D.C."

I stand up stiffly, my muscles protesting the movement. Everything hurts. Not just the rope burns. But my joints. My head. My heart.

I refuse to believe that Jax is dead. I just can't.

We're in a field in the middle of nowhere. A dirt road leads out to the spot. There might have been a barn or something here before. There's a clearing where we stand. The tall brown grasses undulate in the breeze. It's chilly and I shiver despite my leather jacket.

Mark leads us to a sleek gray sports car. "You ladies can take the front," he says.

"Oh, no," Jovana says. "This little troublemaker is sitting in the back with a laser harness."

Mark looks at me with compassion. "It's more comfortable than the ropes," he says.

I have no idea what they are talking about. Mark opens the back door of the car. I slide onto the seat.

Jovana opens the front. "You drive," she says

to Mark. "I have to figure out what Sutherland is up to." She tosses my backpack onto the floor. I wonder if everything is still in it. The ring. My nightie. The weapons and phone. I slowly try to reach for it, trying to avoid getting their attention.

"The alert went out," Mark says as he takes the wheel. "Everything has gone according to plan."

"So Bronson took the fall?" Jovana asks.

"According to the transmission. You want to see it?" Mark punches at the dash.

"Get the girl secure," Jovana says. "And make sure we are cloaked. I don't want anyone following our path."

My fingers brush the strap of the backpack.

"You don't even want the network to see?" Mark asks.

"Not unless we're forced to." Jovana glances back at me. "I want to keep this girl with me and they might intercept."

My hand closes on the bag. I wonder why they would do that. I guess because I'm a special. Jovana must know that.

The bag is closed up, but I pull it next to me on the seat.

Mark glances back at me apologetically. "As

long as you don't make any sudden movements, the grid restraint shouldn't be too uncomfortable," he says.

He notices the bag. "Is she supposed to have that?" he asks Jovana.

"I took the weapons and tech," she says and turns to fix her stare at me. "I left you your tawdry underwear and that tacky ring."

I glance at the bag. At least I have a couple things of my own.

"You'll want to buckle up," Mark says. "It will help you stay still."

I look around for a seat belt, but don't see anything. Then Mark must hit a button, because one slides out from between a gap in the cushions. I tug it around me and snap it into the other side. A red light on the face of the buckle shifts to green.

Instantly, a hundred yellow lines appear across the seat, marking my body with their grid. They flash for a second, then go red.

"What is it?" I ask. I lift my arm and feel a little jolt, a gentle burn.

"Laser restraint," he says. "If you make any sudden movements, it will zap you."

My heart hammers. I move a finger slightly

and feel a warm buzz on my skin. That's not too bad.

"It's like this," Jovana says, and tosses a paper wrapper to the back.

It immediately incinerates in a flash. The smell of smoke chokes me.

"That would be considered a fast movement," Mark says.

"Got it," I manage to cough out.

Mark shakes his head as we pull away from the clearing. He turns on a fan that sucks the smoke under the dash.

"Let's see that transmission," Jovana says.

Mark taps his screen as he navigates the dirt road. I guess auto-drive doesn't work in places like this. Even Vigilante tech can't manage the deep country.

The terrible, awful thought of Jax being dead creeps in on me again. A tear slides out of my eye and rolls down my face. I feel a warmth from the laser catching the movement and warning me with a shot of heat.

Why has Jovana taken me, anyway? I don't know what good I am. Maybe as a bargaining chip. It does seem Sutherland has been blowing her off.

But here's another Vigilante, perfectly willing to help and using all the tech that would register in the network surveillance. He's not trying to hide anything.

His car's dash voice is a commanding male voice. "Identify your prisoner."

Mark glances over at Jovana. "I'm not sure I can avoid a scan on her," he says. "What's the situation?"

"She's a special," Jovana says. "They won't get anything on her. Let them scan. The cloak will keep it from actually transmitting until we go back on grid."

Mark punches at the screen. The laser lines turn off. I think I should make a lunge for the door, but Mark quickly says, "The beam can burn you too. Hold still."

I wait for the line to pass over me, too scared to even breathe. When it's finished, the laser grid flashes back into place.

Jovana busts out with a laugh. "That girl believes anything."

My face burns. I guess the beam wasn't dangerous after all.

Mark watches the screen. "She's just

unfamiliar with all the tech. It's a year's worth of training."

Jovana's face contorts in anger. I guess she doesn't like Mark defending me.

The screen flashes with only my name, like it did in the silo with Jax. No wonder she didn't recognize me in the parking lot. Until I showed up in the car with her watch, she didn't know who I was.

Mark whistles. "They don't even have a last known location on her," he says. "She's up there in the pecking order. That's good, as it means it won't transmit our location."

Mark clicks away my screen. The male voice says, "Prisoner identified. Special is not to be harmed."

He looks over at Jovana. "I assume you're not planning to hurt her?" he asks.

Jovana rolls her eyes. "Whatever. By tomorrow, everything will have changed. The committee meets tonight over the Bronson thing, and Sutherland will have global command by morning." She gestures over her shoulder at me. "First thing, I'll have her special status revoked and we can finish her off."

I don't even react to her wanting to kill me. I want her to talk more about this plan of Sutherland's. It sounds like something big is going down.

"Show me the video now," Jovana says.

"Right," Mark answers. The screen on the dash shows a list, and he clicks on one option.

The gray-haired man who scanned Colette in her car a week ago comes onscreen. Sutherland again. I want to shrink back from his penetrating eyes, but this is just a recording. He isn't actually looking at us. I wonder how you know which is which — a one-way message or a video conversation.

I don't know if I'll ever be trained to find out.

Jovana is rapt as she listens. When he soberly mentions that Mars Bronson has killed a Vigilante in Germany, she claps her hands. "It's all going perfectly," she says with excitement.

But when Sutherland goes on to talk about two other killings, she frowns. "That wasn't supposed to happen yet. There was a timeline. He's rushing it."

The recording ends and the screen returns to a map with red pulsing points.

"What do you think that means?" Mark asks.

"That means something is going wrong," Jovana says.

"You want to contact him?"

Jovana doesn't answer, and I know it's because she doesn't want to admit that Sutherland isn't answering her calls.

"I don't want to blow our cloak," Jovana says.

She's adamant about that. She must be in some sort of trouble and doesn't want anyone she doesn't trust to know where she is.

"You're not cutting me out of the deal, right?" Mark asks. "I'm expecting to be brought in."

Jovana reaches out to caress his shoulder. "Of course you will be," she says. "I won't let the people who help me get left behind."

Mark looks into the mirror and meets my gaze. I hold it steady. I already know what I have to do. If it's so critical that Jovana stay hidden, then I have to blow the cloak. But first I have to know if the car will recognize me, like Jax's did.

These cars are smart and can tell the difference between ordinary conversation and commands that are intended for it. I think it has to do with the forcefulness of your voice, the direction you're speaking, and using command language.

It's worth a shot.

"Find the nearest bathroom," I say, as if it's to them. But the sharply drawn breath makes the laser grid zap my chest. The front of Armond's lovely leather jacket is marred with an etching.

Jovana laughs. "Pee in your pants."

But the car voice says, "Mia Morrow verified." The dash displays a map and points out the nearest rest stops. Since it's registered my status, it knows to listen to me.

"You have to go, love?" Mark asks.

"Cut her out of the command line," Jovana snaps. "Now."

But she's too late. Before Mark can even touch the dash, I've already told the car, "Remove all cloaking levels."

They can rot in hell.

7

JAX

We're only an hour outside D.C. when Sam gets a buzz on the Blackphone.

"Who the hell is that?" I ask. "Who even knows you have that thing?"

Sam ignores me and answers the call. "Have you found her?"

Her who?

"Is it Mia?" I ask.

Sam shakes his head, straining to listen.

Must be they've tracked Jovana. Good. I'll wring her scrawny neck myself. Then I realize what

I'm thinking. I already strangled someone to death because of her.

I can still see the man's face, turning red, then ashen gray. Killed him with my bare hands. No clean, easy Vigilante dart. The messiest, most up-close way to dispatch someone.

I've thought through that fateful night a million times. Jovana's tears and rage, pointing out the man who abducted her and sold her into the sex slave operation. My blind rage and my hands on his neck, squeezing the life out of him.

Only now that I can put together Sutherland's grand scheme does it all start to fit. Jovana was a plant from the beginning. I saw it at the time, that she was different from the other girls in the slave trader's den. I just thought it meant she was plucky, a survivor.

Now I know I was intended to meet her. She was part of a plan.

I first saw Jovana six months before her betrayal. She seemed so young, so naive. She had nothing to do with the network. She was a civilian, at least that's what our records said, reported as abducted from her college campus.

I was orchestrating a low-level sting on a sex

club in my jurisdiction. Two new Phase Threes had uncovered a more elaborate business behind it. Girls were trained to be sold as extremely high-end slaves to wealthy men.

I had to keep the Phase Threes on the job, since they were my in to this secret bonus service. But the underground bunker where the trade was housed was uncharted by the Vigilantes, and we had no idea what they were getting into. I decided to handle this takedown myself to make sure it went like clockwork.

A dozen girls, from late teens through early twenties, wandered the front room of the sex club, accessible to anyone who knew of the place. They were dressed in outfits that varied from schoolgirl uniforms to leather harnesses that hid nothing.

They circled us, smiling, winking, kissing each other, vying for our attention.

We had to go in as customers, and we had to look the part. Wealthy, able to afford anything they had to offer.

I had no intention of busting the sex club for prostitution. This was not illegal to Vigilantes as long as the girls weren't coerced. Now that we had seen how easy the top business was to infiltrate, the regular law enforcement could sort that out.

I wanted access to the girls sold as slaves in the bunkers below. They, we knew, were taken from their homes, often in other countries, and trained as slaves. Most were chemically restrained with heavy narcotics that got them addicted until the training took over.

They became entirely different people. Scarred. Remote. Unable or unwilling to think for themselves anymore. It was a grim business, and we were going to end it.

The two Phase Threes who had been using the club acted the part, looking over the girls, touching them, spanking them. As planned, I stayed aloof, holding back.

A slick, smiling bald-headed man in a gray suit approached them and they pointed to me as if they had no interest in what I wanted.

He came over and extended a hand. "Mr. Phillips," he said, "I'm Fredrick. I received your preferences and accounts. All is in order."

However, he wasn't quite ready to trust me, and the two Phase Threes, his regular customers, were extracted from the girls on their laps. We were all led to an elevator.

My senses were on keen alert. The background and profile that had been sent to the man were flawless. I was a wealthy businessman who owned a private island. A slightly dark past was added to the file, complaints of cruelty by a few women who were discredited. This all led me to appear to be the perfect customer, both able to afford their services and with the means to keep my life private by whatever means necessary.

Our goal was to find the head man, negotiate a price for his most prized woman, taking our time to learn the layout and extent of his scheme.

And then kill him and any of his guards and henchmen on the spot. An explosives team would then come in and blow the whole operation sky high. We already had the fake permits for a demolition and plans for a new construction, so it would seem perfectly legitimate to civilian government.

Neat, tidy, complete.

Our hardest challenge was to get the girls out alive. Regardless, the business practice would end. None of the financial trails we followed led us to believe this business was any bigger than what we saw here.

Not then, anyway.

When the elevator opened, we were led to a wide sitting room. Fredrick sat us down and offered us drinks.

While he moved behind a bar, another man joined us and introduced himself as Amin, the head trainer. I could tell by his dress and demeanor that neither he nor our bald escort was the one we sought.

"Would you like to meet a few of the women?" Amin asked. "Your opinion of them will help us narrow your choices."

"Of course," I said. "Will there be a proper setting?" I knew the bunker must be a labyrinth of rooms, as there was only one door out of this sitting area. We had not been examined for weapons yet, so clearly we had another check to go through before we were even close to the women or their owner.

"Yes," he said. "Would you like to take a drink with them or see them set up in a play dungeon?"

One of my Phase Threes shifted uncomfortably. I was right to have chosen to go on this mission. They weren't ready.

"My tastes are very exacting," I said.

"I have three girls who fit the profile you sent us," Amin said.

"Let me see them all and select one for the dungeon," I said. This way I could get the layout of the bunker.

"Very well," he said. "And what of your companions?"

"They are my bodyguards and scouts," I said. "They don't need to come with me."

"Excellent. You may leave any weapons here with them." He nodded at Fredrick.

This was what I expected. I pulled a standard Glock from my inside coat pocket and laid it on the table in front of the Phase Threes. Everything so far was according to plan.

Fredrick approached the only door and pressed his palm to a lock. The Phase Threes would anticipate this and take necessary measures to ensure that I could make a hasty exit when it was time. None of the men we were meeting were going to survive this day. No one in this sort of business should.

Amin stayed behind, and Fredrick led the way.

The next room was similar in decor and style to the previous. Two sofas, a bar, and this time two additional doors. A beefy man in a black suit stood in one corner. When we entered, he approached and used a wand to check for any weapons.

"So sorry for the inconvenience," Fredrick said. "We must keep our girls safe."

"Understood," I said. None of the dart guns on my body would be found by a metal detector or a pat down. All were encased in very ordinary items. A wallet, a cell phone, a money clip, and a plastic case of tobacco.

I doubted I would need to use them. Everyone here was armed, and I could use their own weapons on them.

"You may meet the girls with no obligation whatsoever," Fredrick said. "If you would like to try one, a deposit will ensure her safety and our continued willingness to do business."

"Transfer what you require from the account," I said.

"Excellent," he said. "That is being handled now." He paused for a second, listening to the earpiece. Obviously the room was monitored.

"Everything is in order," he said. "Let me bring in the girls. You can take one or choose them all for the playroom."

A door to the left slid open and three women demurely walked in. Their appearance and behavior could not have been any more different from the girls in the front room upstairs. They sat with elegance and poise on the sofa. All wore soft white dresses and ballerina flats.

"This is Elise, Ana, and Shantelle," Fredrick said.

"May I talk to them a moment?" I asked.

"Of course." Fredrick gestured to a chair. "Take all the time you need."

I glanced at the bar. "Maybe the ladies would like a little champagne. Would you?" I asked them as I sat down.

They all nodded, gentle smiles that were neither too fake nor too genuine. All had varying degrees of blond to light brown hair. All were slender and medium height. If they could provide three to match this description so exactly, how many women were back there?

"Do you have others?" I asked Fredrick as he moved behind the bar.

"Are these not to your liking?" He paused, his hand on a bottle.

"Yes, but I think maybe I would like one with

63

more color, darker hair."

"Should I send these away?"

I looked over the women. They did not change in expression whatsoever. I hoped the network could find their homes. I hoped they were not so damaged already that even doing that would not help them.

"The one on the end. She is lovely but reminds me of my sister."

Fredrick spoke quietly, and the door slid open again. A new woman walked in, sultry, dark haired, foreign.

"This is Jovana," Fredrick said. "Is she what you were looking for?"

Jovana was unique from the moment she entered the room. Not as well behaved, I could see. Saucy. Sultry. Dangerous.

She headed to the sofa like a tigress. Her white skirt swished around her knees. Shantelle dutifully stood up and headed out the same door. It led to a hall, narrow and white, with additional doors. Perhaps their quarters. I tapped my watch, a code that would provide a rough layout to the Phase Threes plus the explosives team that was at the ready. That sector needed to be checked before the blow.

Jovana sat down, holding my gaze. I felt locked in, like I couldn't look away. Why was she so different from the others?

Behind me, I could hear Fredrick popping a cork. I leaned forward. "I hope you trust me," I said quietly.

The first two girls nodded faintly. Jovana, however, quirked her eyebrow as if in surprise.

Fredrick returned with a tray.

Each girl lifted a glass and took a sip, including Jovana. With Fredrick close and watching, she behaved in the same precise manner as the others.

But she wasn't broken.

"Never mind this," I said. "I'd like to take Jovana to the dungeon." This girl I could reason with, get her out of the way when everything went down. Somehow the life hadn't been trained out of her.

Her eyebrow went up again, but she said nothing.

"Very well," Fredrick said. "Follow me."

We headed out the second door, opposite the one where the girls came from. Fredrick unlocked the palm security and stood aside to let me through.

I paused in front of the panel. "Now this is fancy," I said, and pressed my own hand to it. The panel flashed red, and I jerked away. "Sorry," I said as the door slammed shut.

"It's fine," Fredrick said, and pressed his hand to it again. The door slid open again.

This time I walked through. He hadn't noticed the small device now attached to it, reading the codes and preparing for when I blew all the security. Vigilantes didn't fight fair. Almost all security technology used by civilians was originally created by manufacturers we controlled, to be easily circumvented when needed.

Unlike the stark white hall the girls came from, this one was covered in burgundy satin and trimmed with gold.

On the right side were two doors. On the left, just one. The hall ended about fifty feet down. This was obviously a wing meant for visitors. Cameras recorded our movements.

There were no guards here, which made it a good place to start the action, if needed. I tapped out the information on my watch.

Fredrick palm-pressed the security on this door. It opened to reveal an expansive room filled with all manner of dungeon play. The decor was deep blue, with padded benches, a leather sofa, and a tall four-poster bed. Along the wall were racks of implements, floggers, whips, handcuffs, and blindfolds.

Jovana was apparently trained to behave in a very specific way, as she immediately walked over to an upholstered platform and kneeled, head down, her hands clasped behind her back.

There were no other exits to this room, so it was useless to me. But I had to seem to be interested in this girl to access the offices. Presumably I would meet the man behind the operation, at least briefly, since we were performing such a costly transaction. I would demand it.

"Will you be remaining to supervise our interaction?" I asked Fredrick.

"I will leave you to your privacy," he said.

"And how are the videos disposed of?" I waved a hand at the supposedly hidden cameras embedded in the elaborate pressed-tin ceiling.

"Destroyed once the deals are finalized," he said crisply.

I nodded. "All right."

"Let us know when you are ready for us, Mr.

Phillips." And with a shallow bow, he left the room.

Jovana had not moved from her position.

"You can stand up," I said.

She did as I asked, eyes on me as she waited for my next command.

We were being watched, so I had to act the part. I walked over to the wall and let my fingers trail across the floggers.

"Do you have a favorite implement?" I asked her.

"Whatever Master deems most pleasurable," she said. Her voice was flat, but her eyes danced.

I pulled a black leather paddle from a hook and slapped it on my palm. It felt good and solid.

Her eyes followed me as I approached her with it.

"I would love a demonstration of your domination," Jovana said and stepped off the padded platform. She strode purposefully over to a high bench and bent over it.

I hesitated. I would have expected her to wait on my command.

"How long have you been in training?" I asked her.

She continued to face away as she said, "As

long as I can remember."

Not a real answer. I came up behind her. I couldn't warn her in any way what was to come, when I started to take down the men running this trade. I could only hope to keep her out of harm's way.

As I approached, she reached behind and lifted the back of the white dress, revealing a long expanse of smooth unbroken skin. They took care of their slaves during training, as her thighs and backside showed no sign of scarring.

"Shall I take the dress off?" she asked.

I looked away. "No."

"Please spank me, Master," she said, but her request didn't quite match her tone of voice, which bore a hint of amusement.

I hesitated. I did not want to lay a hand on these damaged girls, although I was quite sure we were being monitored for any behavior out of the norm. I was supposed to be in the market for a slave.

I slid the paddle along her skin, smacking her lightly.

"Harder, please," she said.

I almost did it, as now her voice did sound

convincingly like she wanted it, and I could see a glistening of her arousal. Unnerved by this, by how deep the training could go, I spanked her with one solid strike that made her body shift against the bench.

She sucked in a breath.

I stepped back. "Cover yourself," I said. "Go kneel on your platform."

I had witnessed a lot of things in my Vigilante years, prostitutes, drug dealers, mutilated skin, unmentionable horrors. But seeing this girl, enjoying something not for herself, but because she had been trained to, struck a chord in me.

I wanted her to understand that she had been manipulated. I needed her to want her freedom.

But she had been turned on by this.

Maybe it was her true nature.

Jovana moved across the room and knelt on the platform as I asked. I set the paddle on the bench.

"I've seen enough," I said.

"Are you sure?" Jovana asked. She touched her hands to her shoulders, unfastening some clasp, and the dress puddled around her knees. She was completely naked beneath it.

She didn't want me to discard her. This made sense. The girls were probably expected to make the sale. Perhaps they were punished if they weren't accepted.

My eyes skimmed her. She seemed healthy and unmarked. Even though it was inadvisable, I walked over to her and knelt next to her. "I'm getting you out of here," I said. "You won't belong to anyone."

She took my hand and slid it between her legs to show how slick and wet she was. "I want to belong to you."

I stood up, my anger with the people who had put her in this position reaching a fever pitch. I was ready to find out who was in charge of her. Who had done this to her.

And take him out.

"I want this one," I said to the ceiling. "I'm ready."

Jovana didn't move, surrounded by the cascades of her discarded dress, as Fredrick returned from the door.

"Jovana will give you many years of pleasure," he said. "Shall we meet in our business offices?"

I did not glance back at the girl. There was no way to ensure that she would live if the men here got wild with firepower. But I would do my damnedest.

8

MIA

The dash voice affirms my request to shut off the cloaking level to Mark's Vigilante car. "Cloaking levels removed."

"Cancel!" Jovana shouts. She turns to Mark in the driver's seat. "Jesus Christ. Why did you let her have a command line?"

The dash voice says, "Please clarify the command to cancel."

Mark stabs at the screen. "Restore cloak." He looks at Jovana. "Car control is automatic when the system registers a Vigilante or a special."

"You shouldn't have let her be scanned," Jovana snaps.

"If I had refused, it would have blown the cloak anyway." Mark almost veers off the road as he punches the screen a second time. We're approaching a major highway.

"I don't see why this is such a big deal," Mark says. "Everyone knows we're headed to Washington. Who cares if they track us?"

"I don't want them to track the special," Jovana says.

I know she's lying. Sutherland has cut her off and probably doesn't want her in Washington. She must not want this Mark guy to realize she's been left out.

And they still haven't revoked my command privileges.

"Remove all cloaking," I say.

"Cancel!" Jovana shouts again.

But still, the car says, "Please clarify the command to cancel."

"It's like you've never used a damn car," Mark says angrily.

"I don't let insolent people ride with me," Jovana shoots back.

Mark slams his hand on the wheel. "I told you we had to kill her command line first. She's just going to keep saying commands."

"Revoke Mia Morrow command," Jovana says.

"Revoking command," the voice responds. "Reminder: revocation access of a special must be reported to headquarters."

"No no no," Jovana says. "Do not transmit."

"Cancel revocation of command?" the car asks.

She turns to look at me. "You are more trouble than you are worth."

"Good," I say.

Mark concentrates on the terrain as we bump from the dirt road onto the highway. My body jerks with the motion of the car, and I cringe, expecting a burn from the laser grid.

But I feel nothing. It seems to know what movements are caused by the car and what is something I've done on my own.

I think they've forgotten in their panic that I've removed all the cloaking. I suppress my smile.

"Enough of this," Jovana says. She turns back to the dash. "Kill prisoner."

"What?" Mark shouts. "No! Cancel command."

"Conflicting commands," the voice says. "Control restricted to Vigilante 67309."

Jovana sits back in her seat, angry. "Well, at least only you can command the car now," she says to Mark.

I try to calm my panic. Each rise of my chest makes the lasers buzz me. Would it be that easy to kill me?

"We are not incinerating a special in my car," Mark says. His voice has lost all trace of friendliness. "Now you're starting to be more trouble than YOU'RE worth."

Jovana switches tactics, rubbing Mark on his forearm below the rolled-up sleeve. "This is a bad situation," she says. "I'm glad you're here to manage it."

Surely this Mark guy isn't going to fall for that number. But I can see his shoulders relax. Whatever she's doing, it's working. I start wondering about mood-enhanced speech. What it entails. How it works.

Something seems off about Jovana's hand. Her skin isn't quite right. Does she have one of those fake skins on? Like Klaus used when he poisoned Jax? Is she giving Mark some drug to calm him, make him compliant?

"I'm glad you called me," Mark says.

Gotta be drugged. Nobody calms down that fast.

The dash lights up with a transmission.

"What the hell?" Jovana says. "I thought we were cloaked." She lets go of Mark's arm to stab at the screen.

Mark's recovery is instant. "No, princess in the back here had the last accepted command." Mark looks down at the message. "I'm going to have to take this call before we go off grid again."

"No!" Jovana says. "I don't want them to know where I am."

"Then you better jump out of the car," Mark says, "because I'm not putting my ass on the line for you right now." He punches the screen.

The face that I see on the screen makes my pulse jump. It's Colette! Her information scrolls below, but I can't take my eyes off her face. I can't believe it's her!

"I see you've got some interesting cargo," she says. "How about you let me take one of them off your hands?"

"Don't listen to her," Jovana says. "She's in league with Jax."

"Jax is dead," Mark says. "Isn't that right?"

Colette's face gets serious. "Yes. He was dispatched this morning. It's all been very unfortunate." She looks over at Jovana. "Trust me, I have no desire to take you. It's the special I want."

"You can have her," Mark says.

Jovana smacks at the screen and ends the call. "Initiate all cloaking levels," she says.

"Voice command not authorized," the car responds.

Mark laughs. "You better talk nicer to me," he says.

"Cloak it," Jovana growls.

"Okay, okay," Mark says. "Initiate all cloaking levels."

The car responds. Still, my heart is in my throat. Colette knows where I am!

"So who is this Colette person anyway?" Mark asks.

I want to jump in and say that she is Jax's friend, but I keep silent. If Colette says Jax is dead, doesn't that mean it's true?

But then, why would she want me?

Except to take me back to Jax.

"Just some Vigilante who took an interest in our prisoner a ways back," Jovana says.

"What's so interesting about this girl you've nabbed?"

Jovana shrugs, her hand gripping Mark's arm again. "I was just instructed to bring her with me to Washington and to keep it quiet."

Really? This is the first I've heard of this, although I've been drugged for most of the day with Jovana. Maybe Sutherland talked to her, and I don't know it.

Mark commands the car to go super speed to arrive in D.C. in time for the Vigilante committee hearing.

Mark and Jovana start talking normally again, the argument between them seeming to dissipate. She really must be doing something to manipulate him. Maybe she did it to Klaus too.

And Jax too, back in their day. I doubt it's her sparkling personality that reels them in.

"Show me the footage of the execution," Jovana purrs. Her hand continues to stroke his arm.

Mark pulls up a video. I'm torn between

watching it and staring out the window, unable to cope with the visual of Jax's death.

But I'm a Vigilante now, and I don't believe Colette would have randomly discovered me in Mark's car. She was watching for me. Maybe Sam has been scanning the network for any trace of my identity.

And they wouldn't do that unless Jax asked them to.

The screen shows the inside of a white room. Carter, the guy I met at the Missouri silo, stands next to Jax.

"It's time to go off grid for good," Carter says and clicks an invisible button on the table. A panel slides open, and he lifts a silver case from a hidden compartment.

"You going to fight or can I do this with just us?" he asks.

"I don't need an audience," Jax says.

My heart hurts. He's just standing there, preparing for the end.

Carter pulls out a syringe, and Jovana cheers when he holds it up to the camera to show it is a yellow snuff dart.

"I'd ask for last words, but I don't really give

a shit," Carter says.

"Do what you've got to do," Jax answers.

I watch Jax's eyes. I'm overcome with emotion. I love this man. He's perfectly calm in the face of his own death. I don't think I could ever be nearly so composed and strong.

Carter pricks Jax's arm.

I'm glued to Jax's handsome, perfect face. It's bruised. They must have beaten him after they took him from the hotel. Jax told me they'd take his body to a crematorium. There would be no trace of him left. I'd never see his face again.

But then, I see something that gives me pause. A quick change of expression before the needle is fully in.

Jax crumples his face as the poison hits him. It's not a natural look, at least not to me. It feels scripted.

Then there is a small genuine look of surprise.

"Ha!" Jovana says. "He didn't think they'd really do it!"

Jax falls to his knees, then crashes face-first into the floor. It's all I can do not to cry out, but even the single heave of my chest causes the lasers to singe me again. Maybe I should just flail, fight, let it burn me up.

"Rewind it," Jovana says with a laugh. "I want to see him go down again."

They go back to when Carter injects the drug into Jax. And I see it again, this strange face crumple.

I've seen Jax poisoned. I've witnessed how he reacts. It wasn't a snuff dart then, but I suspect this expression he is doing isn't real. He's done it deliberately.

Like he's faking it.

And suddenly, I know. I know it with the certainty of someone who loves the way I love Jax. If he were truly dead, I would have felt him go.

And despite the fact I've seen him fall to the ground, I know it.

He's not dead.

He's not.

9

JAX

Sam nudges me. He's ended his call. Paulson drives at full speed, flashing by traffic on an interstate now, trying to make good time to D.C.

"What's got you all wrapped up?" Sam asks. "The woman?"

I grunt. "I was just remembering that slave trade bust where I met Jovana."

"She should not have made it out alive from that," he says. "You guys blew up the whole club in the end. Your Phase Threes got the women out of the bunkers, but Jovana wasn't with them."

"Obviously, she was a trained operative from the start," I say.

"Obviously, she was only there to meet you."

We're drawing the same conclusion. In the year I sat in prison, I reviewed all that I knew about her. She hadn't behaved like I would have expected a slave to during that first meeting. And she hadn't been rescued by any of my people in the ensuing chaos.

But she turned up again, not two days later.

"I guess I was supposed to carry her out of there with a background of fire," I say bitterly. "But she found me anyway. Her plan resumed."

"So you think Sutherland hired her early on?" Sam asks.

"No doubt. I just don't know why I was a target." I watch the landscape whiz by. We are probably only an hour outside D.C. at this point.

"We can ask Sutherland when we see him," Sam says. "That will be a friendly chat."

"Who called on your Blackphone?" I ask. "You have more people assembled?"

"Colette," he says. "She found Mia."

My voice explodes in the car. "What? Where is she?"

Sam frowns. "Colette's handling it."

"No," I insist, bringing my tone down. "I will handle it. Where is she?"

"Headed toward D.C., same as us."

"Who is she with?"

Sam fiddles with his phone.

"Sam. Who is she with?"

"The mission is more important than the girl right now," Sam says.

"I decide that. Not you."

Sam sighs. "You're always going off half-cocked."

"Bullshit. I'm never half-cocked."

He shakes his head. "We'll find her in D.C."

"That's not good enough for me." I want her now. I need to see her now. I don't think I even care about the mission anymore. Mia was right back in Nashville. This isn't worth it.

She is what's worth it.

"You're going to have to wait, bro," Paulson says from the front seat. "Put your dick away."

I've had enough of this asshole. In less than a second, I've whipped off my T-shirt and wrapped it around his neck. "Do not go around disrespecting the ladies," I hiss in his ear.

"Engage auto-drive," Sam barks at the car, which has already veered into a new lane.

Paulson clutches at the shirt. I know if he has any training at all, he can tear it away. That wasn't my point. Now that the car has to calculate with traffic, it slows down to a speed that is barely over the legal limit.

"We need to get back on track to get to D.C.," Sam says. "Let the asshole go."

I have no intention of doing that. I want control of this car, or out of it. I need to find out who has Mia and extricate her before any more harm can come to her.

A green sign for the Potomac River whips by. I can see the stretch of blue ahead. We're about to cross it via a bridge on the interstate.

And I make my choice.

Before anyone can notice my actions, I tie the shirt around the headrest, snatch the Blackphone from Sam, and open the car door.

Paulson tries futilely to lock the car down, but I'm on the roof before he can untangle himself from my shirt. I stand, feeling the wind whip around me. If he goes into high speed with me up here, I'm a goner. But the river approaches fast, and without a second thought, I leap from the roof of the car as we go over the bridge.

I can only hope there's enough water in the river to handle this dive.

10

MIA

If Jax is alive, then where is he?

Mark and Jovana seem giddy now after watching the video of Jax's execution. But I can only stare out the window in a bit of a daze. We're driving incredibly fast now, using that Vigilante super speed, and normal civilian cars get left behind as though they are parked on the highway rather than driving alongside.

"So how are you guys going to fake MY death?" Mark asks.

Jovana stops laughing. "Shut up around her."

"Come on, you said that by this time tomorrow, it won't matter," Mark says. "Can I get blown into space? I want something fantastic."

"Don't be ridiculous," Jovana says. "It has to be easy to place in the record."

That explains Klaus, I think. His faked death.

I'm so ready to be out of this car. A dozen muscles are killing me from trying to stay still.

"We should take some side roads," Jovana says. "Probably that do-gooder will be tracking our potential routes by now."

"All right," Mark says. He taps the map on his dash screen. "We'll do a little zigzag."

We exit the interstate and head along the frontage road a while. Then the car makes a dramatic turn onto a small two-lane highway.

"How much time will we lose?" Jovana asks.

Mark fiddles with the screen. "An hour."

Jovana rests her head on the back of her seat. "That's fine. We'll still get there in time."

For what? I wonder. And what do they need me for?

I want to ask, but don't bother. They seem to have forgotten about me for the moment.

A car appears at the crest of the hill ahead,

coming at us with incredible speed.

"That's not civilian," Mark says. A red alert goes off on his dash.

"Shit, I bet it's that girl again," Jovana says. "Can you lose her?"

"Maybe," Mark says. He guns the car.

Colette's image and information come on the dash, filling it this time since she's not on the screen herself.

Colette Rigal

Phase Six Driver

Last Known Location: Missouri Silo

Immediate Commander: Alan Carter

Too bad the car won't listen to my commands anymore. I'd make it stop.

Colette blows past us. I turn to see where she goes, but the laser grid zaps me in twenty places. "Ouch!" I shout.

Jovana laughs. "You don't learn very fast, do you?"

"Is the car coming around?" Mark asks. His eyes are on the rearview mirror.

Jovana swivels in her seat. "Yes. She's turning."

"Damn. She's a Phase Six," Mark says. "She

can outmaneuver me in a heartbeat."

I'll say. I remember how she was able to cut me off when I was walking. She can turn that car on a dime.

Trees and driveways whip by us as we fly along the narrow highway. It's rural here, plantation country, but there are vehicles on the road. Mark's car deftly swerves around a tractor and two pickup trucks.

"Did we lose her?" Jovana asks, peering out the back window.

"Hardly," Mark says. "She's gaining."

We whip around two more cars. One of them blares a horn at our speed.

"Cloaking isn't very effective out here," Jovana says.

"It's afternoon. Visual cloak doesn't work well in full sun." Mark's voice is full of concern. "If she hails us, we have to stop."

I want to ask what he means, but then the dash screen fills with big red words: VIGILANTE HAIL PROTOCOL.

"Don't respond," Jovana says quickly. "I'll take the heat."

Mark glances over at her. "That's a

downgradable offense in the network. I just made Phase Five last month."

"I'll take care of it," Jovana says. "I'll talk to Sutherland."

I decide it's time to play my trump card. "You sure about that? Because from what I've seen in the past twenty-four hours of knowing you, he isn't returning your calls."

The screen flashes again. RESPOND TO HAIL.

Jovana reaches forward and hits something. "I'll do it."

But the dash doesn't change.

"Car won't listen to your voice or respond to your fingerprint," Mark says. He catches my eye in the rearview mirror.

Time to practice my lying techniques by mixing a little false stuff with the truth.

"Jovana called Sutherland last night from a parking lot in Nashville," I tell Mark. "He wouldn't answer." I shift my eyes to her. "You also weren't the first person she called to try to bail her out. The others knew better."

Mark turns to Jovana. "Tell me she's lying."

She clasps his arm. "She's lying. I talked to

Sutherland last night. You can pull the records easily. And who was Sutherland's original recruit? Me. Who got this whole plan started by taking Jax out of the picture?"

Mark relaxes. "All right."

"She's drugging you, can't you see that?" I ask. "I'm not even a Vigilante and I can tell she's using a prosthetic skin with a drug."

He looks down. Jovana withdraws her hand.

Time to finish this up. "You probably want to offload me as soon as you can," I say. "She kidnapped me because she was too desperate and out of choices to deal with any legitimate Vigilantes in the network."

"SHUT UP!" Jovana yells. She almost flings her arm at me, but then remembers the laser grid and jerks her hand back before it crosses the lines.

Mark punches the dash. "Accept hail," he says.

Jovana lets out a rush of air. "Don't make me cut you out of the deal," she says.

But she's too late. The dash reads "Vigilante 07398 requests to commandeer your vehicle. This operative is your superior. Failure to comply will be instantly reported to your silo."

"Don't do it," Jovana growls.

But Mark says, "Accept."

We slow down and roll to a stop on the side of the road. Just ahead is a sign for a farm, the rusting metal pipes forming a rectangular arch over the slats of a cattle guard.

"System under control of Vigilante 07398," the car announces. "Security deactivated."

The laser grids blink, then disappear.

"Great," Jovana says. "Just great."

I let out a long breath. I push aside a piece of hair that fell over my eye hours ago that I'd been unable to move. I rub at the small of my back, where my tension has formed a knot.

The light on the buckle by my hip blinks out. I press the release button and the lock unsnaps. I sit forward on the seat, stretching. It feels amazing.

I turn around to see if Colette is behind us. She's driving the same silver BMW that I rode in when Jax made me go with her after escaping the Missouri silo. My heart warms with the memory, even though I was mad at the time. He can't be dead. I won't believe it. Colette will know for sure. She'll tell me.

But suddenly I don't want to know. I want to

hold on to the hope that he is fine. That what I saw in the video was right, that he was doing it for show. I whip back around, wanting to just keep going, driving forever so I don't have to face facts if he is dead after all.

Jax went down so hard. Is he that good? Could he fake that?

Fear curdles in my belly. Mark and Jovana sit silently up front. She's stewing, arms crossed in front of her body.

"Here she comes," Mark says.

I turn again. Colette closes the door to her car with her hip, a dart gun held out front with both hands. Her dark pixie hair blows around her face. She looks like something from the Roaring Twenties with her pert nose and lined eyes, her body encased in a fashionable low-waisted dress in white and navy.

She makes Vigilantism look good. I am happy to see her, despite my worries about Jax.

"I'll handle this," Jovana says. She fiddles with something on her wrist. I spot the edge of where the prosthetic skin must begin.

"You changing your drug to a poison?" I ask her.

Mark glances down, eyes wide. He grabs at her arm. "You WERE drugging me!"

"It was for your own good," Jovana snaps. "You need to complete this mission well if you want to get anywhere in the new network."

Colette approaches the windows. I know she can't see us, as Vigilante cars have fake windows that make it appear you can see the interior but you can't. She takes one hand off the dart gun and opens the back door.

Sunlight blasts in. Colette takes a step back, the gun out, until she sees me. "Come on, Mia. You're leaving with me."

I grab my backpack and start to slide across the seat, but Jovana decides to make a break for it, opening her door and dashing around the car.

"Colette!" I shout. "Watch out!"

11

JAX

The frigid water bites into my skin. I feel like I'm breaking through ice, even though the temperature is well above freezing.

Despite the recent rains, the river isn't terribly deep, and I almost scrape the bottom with my chest and belly before moving upward toward the light.

I'm actually grateful for the cold as my body slows down, as all the cuts and contusions from Paulson blast like fire as I sluice through the water.

The splatter when I break through the surface is like a million brilliant gems. The fact that I am alive and able to swim through the river weeds and debris blows away any pain.

I'm going to get to Mia.

I clutch the Blackphone in my hand, glad Sam thinks of everything and the electronics are protected. I pause in the reeds beneath the bridge, watching for any sign that someone is coming. Paulson will want to pull off and look for me. Sam, if he's any sort of friend at all, will recognize I'm not interested in their plan and will put him off.

My feet bump against the river bottom and I drag myself out of the water. I'm wearing nothing but pajama bottoms and shoes. The only solution for the cold and my lack of protection is to keep moving.

I jerk the Vigilante watch from my wrist. I am about to chuck it back in the river so they can't track me, but then I pause. It's another way to communicate if I need to. I decide not to burn the bridge I jumped from, and instead of tossing the watch, I fasten it to a tree where I can find it again later if I need it.

I take off in a fast run, away from the interstate and through the dense trees. Everything in the immediate vicinity is woods, lining the shores of the Potomac.

I spot a telephone pole and run beneath the wires where the ground is easier to manage. I know I'll get to some sort of landmark soon enough where I can contact Colette. It should be the last call on this Blackphone, although I know how to reach her from memory.

The wind blasts my face, and I begin to relax into the run as my muscles warm up. I feel better than I have in a long time despite the fact that I'm half-naked, running in dress shoes, and have nothing on me but a secret phone.

I'm getting closer to Mia.

I'm going to walk away from all this. Sutherland. Jovana. The network. I don't need it. I don't want it.

I want her.

We can figure out what sort of life we want to have. We can do anything. Live on a boat. Or maybe not, with her parents' history.

Get a place in Paris. Or the Swiss Alps. Venice. Or just travel.

As long as I'm with her.

I approach a highway. I cut alongside it, staying in the trees. When I feel I've put enough distance between myself and the bridge, I stop running and let my breath slow down. Time to contact Colette.

I run the phone through several encryption channels and dial her number.

It immediately cuts out, no answer.

I frown. Where is she?

I take off in another jog, worry nipping at my heels. Sam said she had located Mia. I wonder if someone has come after them. I don't know who had Mia to begin with, how she was found. Anything that happened to her after I left the hotel is completely unknown. Those Vigilantes assured me she'd be safe, but if Colette had to track her down, that means she *needed* tracking down.

Where the hell has she been all day?

And where are they now?

I run faster.

12

MIA

Jovana doesn't come around the back of the car like I expect, but flips her way to the roof and back down, landing right on Colette.

Shit, she's good.

"Watch her arm, Colette!" I say. "Don't let her grab you with that poison skin!"

The two of them scrabble on the ground. I drop my bag and circle them, kicking Jovana when I can get a shot in and making sure she doesn't wrap her hand around Colette. I don't want to jump into the fray since Colette is trained and I might get in the way.

Mark gets out of the car with a dart gun and before any of us can do anything, he shoots both Jovana and Colette.

"What the hell?" I say, lunging for him.

"Back off," Mark says. "I don't know what is going on here, but I'm not going down for it."

"Jovana kidnapped me," I say quickly. "I don't know why. She couldn't get Sutherland to listen to her, and Klaus isn't answering calls."

"Why is this Vigilante Colette so intent on getting you?"

"She's a friend of Jax. He'll want me."

"But he's dead."

I don't say anything, and he curses under his breath. "Sutherland's not as solid in his plan as he would let us believe," he says.

"What is his plan?" I ask, mentally trying to keep track of the minutes. Jovana and Colette will need an antidote if Mark used a Vigilante poison. Neither of them are unconscious, but clearly struggling with whatever he gave them, breathing heavily on the ground.

"Hell if I know," Mark mutters.

"Are you going to give them antidotes?" I ask,

my voice shaking.

He turns and kicks at his car. "This is fucked up."

"What did you hit them with?"

Jovana starts convulsing, her stomach heaving like she's going to throw up.

"The gastrointestinal one. It's a torture drug." He frowns.

"Well, get the antidote!" I say.

Colette starts to writhe on the ground as well. But still, Mark doesn't move.

I stride over to him and punch him in the belly. "Do it now," I say.

He doesn't even flinch from the blow, but it does take him out of whatever pissed-off daze he's in. He walks to the trunk and opens the lid.

"If you're so keen on waking them up to fight again, you do it," he says. He tosses me a red vial.

"I need two," I say, but then turn away. I'll dose Colette. He can worry about Jovana.

I yank the protective cover off the needle and stab Colette in the arm. The lovely navy and white dress is dusty and torn. Her short bob covers her face.

I drain the antidote into her and kneel down,

the asphalt biting into my knees through my jeans.

Every day since I met Jax has been nothing but the most insane collection of events.

Colette shudders, her hand moving to her belly. Her eyes flutter open. "*Putain, ça douille.*" Her face is contorted.

"You okay?" I ask. I brush her hair back.

"I think I'd rather be dead," she says.

Next to us, Jovana's breathing is labored and pained. She lets out a long terrible groan.

Mark stays at the back of the car, leaning on the upraised lid of the trunk.

"You going to take care of her?" I ask. "You can't let her die. She's a special."

"I'm deciding," Mark says.

Colette pushes to a sitting position. "You had to use *la putain de* belly dart."

"Sorry," Mark says. "It was preloaded."

"Stick to the green one," Colette says, her hands still pressed to her stomach. "Much more civilized."

Mark shrugs.

I stand up and help Colette to her feet. She staggers a bit, and I wrap an arm around her waist.

"Jax is going to be glad to see you," she says.

"Shit, I should have known," Mark says and kicks the car again.

It takes a moment for their words to sink in, but then my heart leaps. "He's alive?"

Colette takes a step toward her car. "Yes. He's with Sam. They're on their way to Washington." She points to the bag. "Is that yours?"

I snatch it up. My heart is hammering. Jax is alive! I knew it! I want to scream it out loud, but I just hang on to Colette as we hobble across the broken asphalt.

We make it to the BMW and she rests her hand on the hood. "I'm not ready to drive yet."

"Let me," I say. "I've handled a couple Vigilante cars at this point."

"Not one for a Phase Six you haven't," she says with a pained laugh.

"First time for everything."

She lurches toward the passenger side, and I help her get in the seat. "This one takes an hour to recover from," she says. "Not, as you say, *my first rodeo* with this dart."

"Just rest a bit," I answer and close her door.

I go around to the other side. Colette has already started the engine, and it scarcely even vibrates beneath my seat as I slide into place. I toss my bag in the back.

Colette's steering wheel isn't a circle like other cars. It is made of two triangles with a rounded outer grip. It doesn't just turn, but also tilts forward or back.

"You might be right about this," I say.

"You'll get it," Colette says, pressing the side of her head to the cool glass of her window. "I'll talk you through it. Once you have the basics, we can do auto-drive. I just want to make sure you can manage the car if we drop out of it."

In front of us, Mark has bent down next to Jovana. He's holding another red antidote vial, but he hasn't given it to her yet.

"Shouldn't we bring her in or something?" I ask.

"Can't. She's a special. And I'm not combat trained. It was everything I had just to put up a defense." Colette's normal French lilt goes darker, like she's defeated. "I don't know how we can take her out of commission."

"Are you still in good standing with the Vigilantes?" I ask. "I think I may have gotten Sam in trouble."

"He was decommissioned. Technically I'm still on duty, but until all this settles out, none of us are really safe." She points at the steering wheel. "The gearshift is by your right thumb. Click and hold the top button to go into reverse."

I do what she says.

"You can press the gas like normal with your foot," she says, "but be careful about pulling the wheel toward you. That doubles your acceleration."

"Is the brake like normal?" I feel around the bottom with my foot.

"Yes, there is a standard brake. But you can also stop the car instantly by jerking down on the wheel with deliberate force."

"Okay," I say. "Anything really stupid I could do?"

"Don't mess with the switch on the base of the steering wheel. It is for the other modes of the car and changes all the actions of the buttons and wheel motions."

"Like when you drive across water?" I ask.

"Yes, like that."

I take in a deep breath. Mark still hasn't moved from his position beside Jovana.

I ease the accelerator down, half expecting this

specialized car to shoot backward like a rocket. But it rolls the way a civilian car would. I let go of my held breath.

Colette laughs lightly. "You look like you're strapped to a missile."

I press the brake. "I feel like I am. Which one for drive?"

"Go with the bottom one. It's the equivalent of the automatic transmission in civilian cars."

I press it. I check the mirrors. There's no one coming. In fact, no one has passed us the entire time we've been out here. "What happened to the traffic? Surely there are at least a few cars along here."

"I had a couple locals set up a construction detour," Colette says. "The way that jerk was driving, he was going to kill a civilian."

I pull out onto the road with a tentative push on the gas. Jovana still writhes on the ground. Mark has at least uncapped the antidote.

As we come up beside them, Colette rolls down her window. "Civilians arriving any minute. Clean this up."

Then we are past and the two of them get smaller and smaller until I can't make them out anymore.

We approach a big orange and white roadblock. A few bewildered neighbors are standing beside this as if they don't understand why it's there. They're even more confused when we swerve around it and move on.

"They'll figure it out and move it," Colette says. "We have to get to Jax." She taps on her dash screen. "Uh-oh."

I glance down at it, my hands tight on the wheel. "What?"

"I got a call from Sam's Blackphone while we were tied up with Jovana."

"Is there a message?"

Colette shakes her head. "I'm using an encrypted line, off network. Voice mail isn't secure."

She dials through. The pinging sound makes me shiver as the call tries to connect.

It picks up, the screen showing only an audiowave that rises and falls with the sounds.

But I'd know that voice anywhere.

"About time you bothered to answer," Jax says. "You getting your nails done?"

Colette laughs. "Got a red dart to the belly," she says. "Think I'll choose a polish to match."

"Ouch," he says. "Hate the red darts."

He pauses, and I can barely contain myself. I want to squeal but I don't want to interrupt them.

"I could probably use a lift," he says. "I jumped off the Interstate 81 bridge into the Potomac."

"Jax!" I cry out. "Are you okay?"

"Mia?" he asks. "You have Mia?"

"I do," Colette says. "I'd laugh but it really hurts when I laugh."

"We'll pick you up," I say quickly. "I'm driving Colette's car until she recovers from the dart. Where are you now?"

His voice is warm now, happy sounding. My heart skitters. I can't believe I'm talking to Jax!

"I'm running along Route 63. There's a funeral home ahead, but it's not on the Vigilante books. So I'll head into the cemetery behind it."

"Got it," I say. "How far are we?" I ask Colette.

"If I can coax Mia into super drive, we'll be there in thirty," Colette says. "She's never driven like a Phase Six before, though."

Jax chuckles. "She hasn't driven like a Phase Six *yet*."

"We'll be there in thirty," I say, and simultaneously slam the accelerator and pull the wheel toward my chest.

I'm getting *Jax*.

13

Jax

I really could use a shirt.

A little old lady sitting on a concrete bench near the entrance to the cemetery watches me curiously as I enter through the pedestrian gate. I wish I had put on workout shorts and running shoes when I left the hotel, so I could just jog past her and seem perfectly normal.

But I couldn't have predicted that I would end up strolling through the manicured grounds of the final resting places of so many fine souls when I got hauled out at gunpoint.

I nod at her kindly, feeling her gaze as I stroll past. Despite my state of dress, I feel I'm better off inside the walls than walking randomly along the highway.

Mia and Colette should be here soon anyway.

Mia!

I'm already restless with plans. We'll stop for clothes, have a decent meal, then I'll grab some identification from my nearest stash — not D.C., but somewhere — and rent a car. A plain old civilian car! I'll shut down my known residences, or maybe I won't even bother, just fly to Switzerland and buy a chateau at whatever point is the farthest from any Vigilante silo.

Forget they exist. Forget anything else exists.

Mia. All to myself. Endlessly. I stop in front of a row of well-nursed chrysanthemums. We'll garden. We'll grow flowers and vegetables.

We'll be normal people.

Avoid boats. Big bodies of water. Guns. Poison darts.

Buy lots of rope. Practice knots. On each other. Endlessly.

Maybe I'll lead a Boy Scout troop.

The thought makes me laugh. Everything

makes me laugh. I'm out. I'm done. It doesn't matter.

It's over.

The elderly lady has taken out an apple and is slicing it. She alternates eating one slice and setting another in the grass by a headstone. Her simple joy in doing this calms me.

Mia and I are going to be just like that. Quiet. Devoted. A love affair that even death can't end.

I cross the lawns to get closer to the road. There's another concrete bench under a tree that can hide me from casual glances.

I sit on it. Opposite is a double headstone with two overlapping hearts. Doris and Bernard Thatcher. They died within weeks of each other after long eighty-something-year lives.

That's what I want. That exactly.

Now that I'm not running, the chill sets in. But it feels good. I feel good. The jump and the swim and the race away from the river have cleared my head and body from the drug that got me out of the silo.

I breathe in deeply, loving the clear crisp air and the glory that is autumn in this part of the country. The leaves are already changing and soon will be bright with reds and golds.

I'm getting a new start, right here.

I feel something brush my arm, and I leap into action, ready to fight.

But it's the old lady.

"So sorry to startle you," she says. "I thought you could use this." She passes me a soft, well-worn cardigan, the sort an older man might wear.

"It was my husband's." She waves her hand in the direction of the bench where she was sitting when I passed. "I've been silly, bringing him snacks and sweaters. I think it would look very fine on you. He'd like that."

My mind wants to examine her story for inconsistencies, lies, or attempts to detain me while someone comes for me. I can't quite program out my distrust, my trained responses.

But I force it down. This is my new life. I slide an arm into the sleeve of the cardigan. It smells of hand-washing and home.

"Thank you," I say. I plan to make up a story, some bit of cover for why I'm out here dressed this way.

But she just pats my arm. "I've seen people come out here in all states. Grief does that." She steps away. "The sweater looks good on you."

Then she starts walking, not back to the grave, but toward a single car parked along the road.

I sit back on the bench. Mia would be that sort of woman, I think, one who would let go of a beloved article of clothing to help someone else. "You picked a good one," I say to the sleeve, as if it's the person who once wore it. "So did I."

The old lady's car chugs past at a snail's pace. She waves as she passes by. I lift my hand in return.

This has been the slowest half hour of my life. But I think it might be one of the best. I know what I'm doing now. Where I'm going. I don't have to run the U.S. syndicate. I don't need to track down criminals or lead a silo. I've experienced enough crime-fighting in this lifetime already to have done my part.

I'm going to settle down.

My brother, who opted out of the network when I went in, has three kids. I can have some, let them get to know their cousins. I'll teach them martial arts. Coach Little League.

By the time Colette's silver BMW appears at the gate, I have my entire life figured out. I just need to start it.

I assume Mia is driving, by the lurching acceleration and brakes. She's coming through the cemetery at a crazy clip.

Slow down, I think, and stand up to meet them. Hopefully she won't plow into the trees.

The car slams to a stop. The door opens and Mia appears. I'm so thrilled to see her that at first I don't really think about how she's acting. She's bruised and her cheekbone is purple. Rage surges in me that Jovana even touched her.

She runs over to me and flings herself into my arms. I hold on to her so tight. She feels perfect.

I lean back to tell her what I've planned, our new life, just like what she talked about in the hotel in Nashville, when I'd been foolish and insisted that my job was more important than our future.

But her face is frantic, panicked. "Get in the car. Colette's feeling well enough to drive now. We're in a terrible hurry."

She drags me by the hand back to the car.

I resist, digging my feet in. "Wait. I haven't even kissed you!" I don't understand her rush. "We're together now. We don't have to go with Colette if you don't want to."

Mia doesn't seem to be listening. She tugs at

me and notices my naked wrist where the cardigan sleeve is a little short. "Where is your Vigilante watch? That's why Sam couldn't find you. Come on!"

I refuse to move. "Mia, stop. I don't want to go back there. I don't want to drive fast or head to Washington." I reel her in, pulling her close again.

For a moment she looks up at me, her eyes meeting mine. I think I've gotten her to see what I'm talking about. That this is *our* time now.

"Jax!" she says with exasperation. "We have to GO. They're going to execute three Vigilantes on camera within hours."

"They chose the wrong side, then," I say. "I'm out of the game. I just want to go somewhere with you."

She hesitates. "Jax, I don't think you understand. Everything has gone wild. And they've put out a kill order on Sam and Colette."

14

MIA

What has happened to Jax?

He stands in the middle of the cemetery, wearing a worn-out cardigan and pajama pants, refusing to get in the car.

He's looking out over the grounds.

I tug on his hand again. "Did something happen to you, Jax? We can't stay here. We're within minutes of our last known location." I glance up at the sky. "There could be a helicopter or a satellite trace anytime now."

Jax's face is still screwed up, as if he's trying

to understand what I've said. "Who put the kill order on Colette and Sam?" he asks.

"Sutherland," I say with exasperation. "We think his plan wasn't working and he got desperate." I jerk on his arm. "Can you please get in gear?"

He lets me lead him to the car. I jerk open the door and climb in the back. I don't want him to be far from me. Something's changed in him, and we need to figure out a plan.

"Now that is a fashion statement," Colette calls back as Jax sits behind her.

Jax nods absently.

"Is he okay?" Colette mouths into the rearview mirror as our eyes meet. I just shrug.

"Hold on to your seat belts, lovebirds," she says. "We're going to see what this baby can do."

"They'll see your speed," Jax says. He shakes his head as if he's clearing his mind.

"Not if I'm in the trees," Colette responds in singsong.

She slams on the accelerator and the car whips around to blast back out the cemetery gates.

I turn to Jax. "Are you all right?"

"Yeah." He leans forward to look at the screen. It still flashes with the alert on Sam and

Colette. "How long since that went out?"

"Ten minutes," Colette says. "I figure that was about when Jovana got her antidote and took over the situation." She glances back at us with a frown. "Vigilante blood is spilling all over the globe."

She guns the car and we fly along the highway. She swaps the screen out for a map with red pulsing dots. "Nobody's that close," she says. "And nobody's heading for us." She presses a few buttons. "But I'm not taking any chances." The dash goes dark as she returns to cloaked mode.

Jax and I fall against the back of the seat as she jets forward and veers off the road. We go straight into the trees and she dodges the big ones, weaving through spaces I don't think we can possibly fit.

After a moment, my body adjusts to the erratic movements. I try to calm down. I've been in a panic ever since I saw the alert.

Jax stares out the window. He still seems to be in some sort of daze.

"You went down hard when they shot you with that dart," I say to him. "Were you faking that?"

"No," he says. "They drugged me enough that

I would pass for dead." He turns back to me and his eyes soften. "I'm fine now."

"You don't seem fine."

His jaw tightens.

I wrap my fingers around his hand, squeezing. "We're going to try to intercept Sam. We think it's safest if we all stick together."

"Is Paulson still with him?"

"No. They had to separate or Paulson couldn't stay in the game."

This gets him. He sits up. "Is Sam safe?"

"He'll get by," Colette calls back. "He's got his toys."

Jax sets a Blackphone on the console. "You can reach him with this."

"Yes, he mentioned it in the last communication. Said you'd taken it from his hand before jumping into the river." Colette's laugh is like the tinkle of glass. "You are one crazy man."

"Where are we going?" Jax asks.

"D.C. Same as everybody," Colette says. "It will take an hour since I have to evade."

Trees continue to whip by, but they are thinner now, and the car jostles less.

"Sam is coming up with a plan," she says. We

arrive at a small road, and Colette gets on it. "That should have killed a visual if they had it. I'll do another maneuver in a bit just in case." She sets the car on auto-drive and turns around.

"I still have another of your suits in a bag back there," she says. "So you can restore your usual spiffy appearance." She presses a button and a wall rolls up between the front and back seats. "To protect your modesty. Or my virgin eyes." She laughs again.

The wall fits into place, and we can't see her anymore.

I'm not sure what is going on with Jax, but I'm sure he'll feel better in decent clothes. I unzip the bag. "Colette really watches out for you," I say as I pass him a shirt and pants.

Jax stares at the clothes like they're foreign objects. "She always has," he says absently.

I clutch the garments in my lap. "Can you please tell me what is going on with you, Jax? You're not acting anything like the last time I saw you."

His eyes fix on me, drinking in my face, my hair, and roving down my body. I see where he lingers and my blood starts to beat, heating up all the places his glance touches.

He reaches out and slowly, gently, traces a finger along the furry edge of my collar, then up my jaw and across my cheek. "I'm so relieved to see you," he says.

"Me too," I say and close my eyes. He's acting so different from before. But this tender gaze, this slow touch, it's driving me crazier than his passionate wildness.

"Come here," he says, and his arms come around me, dragging me tight against him.

I can barely breathe, so many emotions are competing for attention. Need. Relief. Joy. Excitement. Confusion.

I want to connect with him. I lift my face, expecting the crushing torment of his blazing kiss.

But I get gentle instead. His mouth is tender, soft nibbles that caress my mouth. This glow starts in my belly, something so different from what I felt before. Instead of the passionate flare, it's a feeling of unfurling, like a flower opening. It's intense and full of longing.

Jax deepens the kiss then, parting my lips. His hands are everywhere, my waist, my back, my hips, like he needs to memorize my shape. Like he can't believe it's really me.

I turn in to him. The cardigan is soft and smells like fresh laundry, air-dried in a backyard. I suddenly understand the need to touch him, to make sure he's real. It's like we're in some other world, and we're not sure what senses to trust.

I run my hands along the soft sweater, feeling his biceps as they expand into his shoulders. I begin to unbutton the front, wanting more of him, to feel every muscle.

His belly is hot and flat and firm. I run my hands up his smooth chest. I can feel his every inhale.

Jax slides his hands under my bottom and lifts me, pulling me in front of him. My knees go on either side of his thighs and I'm spread wide. His pajama pants hide nothing, and I can feel how erect he is. I reach down and pull him free, rock hard in my hand.

"Jax," I whisper, feeling heat rush down below. I need him terribly. No one can see through Vigilante windows. Colette probably put the wall up just for this.

I slide down between his knees and take him in my mouth. His pelvis rises up. I take in all I can, reveling in his hot flesh, slightly salty.

His hands grasp my head. I move, tentatively, out to the tip and down again. I want to do all the things with Jax. Everything there is to do. In cars. In hotels. In hayfields.

He lifts me up and jerks open the button to my black leather pants. In an instant, he has pushed them down. I kick off my boots so I can be free of the restraints of clothes.

He unzips the front of my jacket and slides it off my shoulders. The gray turtleneck blinds me for a moment as he lifts it past my face. Then the cool air hits my shoulders, and it's away, tossed against the window.

I jerk the cardigan away from his arms and peel it down his back. For a moment, he's caught in the sleeves, and I like it, planting a hot kiss on his mouth.

Then his arms are free and he's unfastened my bra, dragging it off me.

He lifts me against him, his lips encircling a breast. His breath is like fire against the tender nipple. One of his hands reaches between my legs, pushing aside the panties as he presses a finger up inside me.

I moan, grinding against him. This has been the longest, most terrible day, but here we are, together, naked skin to naked skin.

His rhythmic strokes become more insistent, more powerful. I'm spiraling up, needing him, wanting to let go of my control. I want to be lost, just for a moment, and let Jax take over my body.

I lift my knee and push the leg of the panties down and over my ankle so I can rock against him freely. I feel his erection against my thigh and don't want to wait for it, but slide down on it. Jax shifts his fingers to massage me as I take him all the way in. I'm on fire, wanting it fast and hot and hard.

Jax squeezes one hip while his hand continues its massage. I lift over him, then slam down, letting him rip through me.

I want to scream, but spare Colette of that and bury my face in his damp hair. Jax works me harder, holding me tight, and lets me pound against him at my own pace.

I'm not going to have to wait for the release I need. Jax's fingers dance along my tender swollen nub, and the fiery thrust of my body over his makes my muscles clench around him. I can't keep quiet then, and cry out, the shudders of my climax starting to ripple out.

I hear Jax groan and feel the hot flow of him inside me. Reality splinters, as all I can feel is the powerful contractions of the orgasm and the tightness of his hand on my hip.

My hands grip his shoulders, the only tether I have as everything else is lost. Jax's arms come around me, clasping me against his hard chest. I can't quite stop, still lifting and dropping down, squeezing against every last rhythmic pulse. I don't want it to end. I want to stay here, locked in this private space, the trees flying by, the world just a hurtling blur of color.

My Jax is back, strong arms pinning me to him. I can barely breathe, the world settling in again. My skin is damp and sizzles with his closeness.

"I've got you," he says against my neck.

I can't speak. I just hold on to him. Life is going to intrude very soon. For this moment, I just want to hang on.

15

JAX

Mia has just zipped up her jacket when Colette buzzes us from the front of the car. "Arriving in D.C. in about ten minutes. I'm going to do some evasive maneuvers to make sure we're cloaked as we go into the belly of the whale."

"You can bring down the screen," I tell her. "Your virgin eyes are safe."

"If you say so!" Colette says, but she buzzes the wall down, filling the car with additional light.

"Let me get your cuffs," Mia says.

I extend an arm and let her fold back the

sleeves and fasten them with onyx cufflinks.

It's a small gesture, but I've never let any woman dress me in any fashion. So it speaks to me. We're going to have to go in and do this thing.

But I swear we're retiring after we take down Sutherland and get this kill order off Colette and Sam.

"The skies are hot hot hot," Colette says as we hop on the freeway toward downtown. She leans forward to peer out. "Three cloaked Vigilantes and at least a dozen fake news choppers."

"How do you spot a cloaked helicopter?" Mia asks. "I can see the ones with big channel numbers on the sides, but nothing else."

"You learn to spot the warping of the scene that indicates a visual cloak." I point out the window. "See that black News 37 one? There's a cloaked one at five o'clock from it."

Mia makes a circle in the air as if she's drawing an invisible clock. "There's a cloud with an unusual bend to it," she says. "I think I see it."

I sit back. "Colette, do we have any sort of plan?"

She glances over her shoulder. "Sam does. We'll go over things when we get together."

"No time to fake your death or his, I guess," I say.

"Gawd, there is no telling who is really alive or dead at this rate," Colette says. "I've never seen the network in this sort of chaos."

"That's exactly the sort of thing you want to create if your intent is to take over," I tell her. I reach for Mia's hand. I haven't forgotten that she doesn't know who she is. I want her to have that information before we go in.

"Did you leave the oval ring at the hotel?" I ask.

She reaches down for a backpack at her feet. "No, I brought it." She pulls out the blue nightie and searches along the bottom of the bag.

I take the wisp of fabric. "I'm glad you rescued this."

She grins, a hint of a blush tinting her cheeks. "Here it is." She holds out her palm. The oversized stone gleams black.

I take it from her and slide it on her thumb. "We'll have it resized for you," I say.

She holds up her hand to examine it. "Okay. Is it important?"

I take her fingers in mine. "It belonged to the

very first Vigilante. His name was Prescott Adams. This ring was given to him by President Eisenhower after World War II."

Mia turns her hand to look more closely at the ring. "Did you find out whose initials are inside?"

"A woman's. The Vigilantes were started by Eisenhower, a global enterprise in honor of his affection for a young woman who drove him around during the war when he was general."

"Did they have an affair?"

"No one knows the sordid details, but everyone is certain they were very close."

"Is she KHS?"

"Yes."

"How does this connect to me?" she asks. Her eyes shine, reflecting the changing landscape outside the window.

"This ring is assigned to you. You are the last surviving member of Prescott Adams's family. The last of the original Vigilantes."

She exhales long and slow. I realize I've gotten ahead of myself with my own plan. In the cemetery when I decided to escape all this, to live a simple life with Mia, I forgot something important.

To ask her what *she* wants.

She presses her fist to her chest. "So I can be a Vigilante if I want to?"

"I don't know. We don't know why you were at the safe house. We don't know what happened to your parents. I think you were being protected."

"How do I find out?"

"A couple committee members would have private, personal knowledge of your history, as they would have voted on your designation as a special."

I let her absorb all this. Her chest rises and falls with each deep inhalation.

"We're about to rendezvous with Sam," Colette says quietly. She understands the implications of what I've said as well.

"Is this why I could go around the silo wherever I wanted?" Mia asks.

"Probably."

"Does that mean I can get into this big meeting coming up with Sutherland?"

I realize she has a very good point. "Quite possibly."

She lets go of me and leans forward, holding on to the back of the front seat.

"It sounds like I have the keys to the kingdom," she says to Colette. "Give me some weapons and let's cause some damage."

Colette breaks out in a wide smile. "Sam's already on it."

16

MIA

A Vigilante.

Me.

I'm still trying to get used to the idea. I don't like the oval ring on my thumb, so I start unraveling the hem of Jax's discarded pajama pants until I have enough thread to wind through the ring and tighten up the hole.

"Just like they used to do in the 1950s with high school rings," Jax says.

"Exactly," I say. I slip the ring on my middle finger. It fits better now.

We drive through the traffic-heavy streets of D.C. Colette has to remove the visibility cloak, or we'll get run over by roaring taxis. We can only hope the other methods to hide us will hold.

The city is thick with cars, and the air bustles with helicopters. Of all the places to meet, this one feels the most fraught. "There's so much security," I say to Jax. "How do we know who is friend or foe?"

"Assume they are all the enemy," Jax says. He sorts through Colette's Vigilante stash of weapons and passes me a dart gun. "You good with this?"

"Well, it's not as hot as the blue one with bullets," I say, teasing.

Jax's gaze drops to my lap, as if he's picturing the metal barrel sliding between my legs. "We're going to have to do that again," he says.

I curl my arm around his neck. "Mmmm-hmmm."

"Okay, lovebirds, Sam at two o'clock," Colette says. "Look lively to see if anyone spots him."

"They'll never get a heat signature in this snarl," Jax says. He scans the perimeter of the car. "Give us a topside view," he says.

Colette presses a button and a panel slides

open to reveal a roof window. "I'm cloaking it because this tech will give us away," she says.

"It's just until he's in," Jax says. He keeps an eye on the helicopters above.

Sam himself appears, taking jaunty steps in a crosswalk ahead with a stream of pedestrians. He lingers near the back of the group, falling behind. When he spots the BMW, he cuts around a taxi and jumps into the front of the car.

"Nobody's homing in," Jax says. "Welcome back, Sam."

He turns in his seat. "Good to see you in one piece, sir." He elbows Colette. "Don't open that roof hatch or he might go jumping off the flyover."

"Hey, Sam," I say.

"Lookin' good, Mia," he says. "Let's bail on this traffic."

"You got something I can use for navigation?" Colette asks. "We've been dark since West Virginia." She buzzes the roof closed.

"I made a stop by one of my hacker networks," Sam says. "I have an off-grid hookup to the Identipad system, plus we can tap into all the V-cars in this jurisdiction who are Phase One to Four. Then we'll know who's around us."

"Young Vigilantes are heavily monitored," Jax explains. "There's a whole channel devoted to chatter about their progress."

"Easy hack," Sam says.

"That's a decent start," Colette says.

"Yeah, the real danger is in the Phase Tens on the prowl," Sam says. "They are going to be like silent ghosts."

"Any kill orders go out other than yours?" Jax asks.

"Not in the U.S. syndicates," Sam says. "We're still part of the alleged cleanup from your indiscretion. But they are putting marks on the Vigilantes taking the fall for the murders overseas."

"How do we know those murders aren't faked?" Colette asks. "They broadcasted Jax's and his wasn't real."

"We don't know it," Sam says. "Nobody can trust anybody for anything."

"Maybe I'm dead right now," Colette says with a laugh. "I don't even know who I work for anymore."

"Me," Jax says authoritatively. "You work for me. And nobody's going to die today. Real or imagined."

Sam shakes his head. "I hope so. I really do."

"So let me get this straight," Colette says. We're stopped again. "Sutherland recruits the foreign Phase Tens, has them do their dirty business in their homelands, and then uses this to fuel a network-wide panic so he can come in and fix it all?"

"He's already been granted access to five other networks," Sam says.

"Why is that a big deal?" I ask. I don't understand why Sutherland is doing this or why anybody cares.

"One of the beauties of the network has always been its syndicate autonomy," Jax says. "We aren't affiliated with any country or government. And each part of the network has its own rules, based on where they live."

"Things that won't fly here might be the norm in Syria or with an African tribe," Sam says. "And others are far more stringent. Most of them aren't nearly as lenient about gunplay as the U.S. is."

"And that's the way it should be," Jax says. "There is no one-size-fits-all justice. And nobody needs to have all the information in one place. It isn't necessary or wise."

Sam pulls a panel off Colette's dash and cuts a couple wires. "Sutherland is gunning for a global network. And now it's starting to look like a good idea, thanks to his own sabotage."

"Where is Carter?" Colette asks.

"Picked up ten minutes ago," Sam says. "Paulson too. They should have had a body ready to cremate. Easy to figure out Jax wasn't disposed of. Sloppy, sloppy."

He twists a new set of wires in and the dash lights up. The map glows red.

"*Mon Dieu*," Colette says. "And that's just the young ones?"

"Half the network is in town," Jax says. "That can't be good."

"I hope Sutherland really is behind this," Sam says. "If he's not, then someone could take out a huge chunk of the U.S. operatives in one go."

Jax sits back, his finger passing over his lips as he gets lost in thought. "This is making me wonder if Sutherland chose Jovana, or if maybe she chose him."

"I don't think so," I say. "She was outraged when he wouldn't call her back. She's pretty much showing up without his permission."

Sam glances back at us. "Looks like you spent some quality time with her." His gaze shifts to Jax. "In fact, you both look like bloody hell."

"We're a little worse for wear," Colette says. "You, however, don't have a scratch on you."

"I'm too intellectual for all this brutality," Sam says. He passes a dart gun back to Jax. "Note that this one is a new drug. No antidote. Wears off on its own but drops them in six seconds. Keeps them down for two hours."

I wonder if that's what Jovana gave me, twice.

"How many of these you got?" he asks.

"Just the one gun. But it has three darts."

I hold the dart gun Jax gave me with both hands, extending my arms so I can find the sights to aim. Jax takes it and passes me the new one. It is lighter and more streamlined. I lift it to check the sights.

Jax raises my elbows so I'm more level. "It has a laser sight." He clicks a button and a red beam hits the window, indicating where the dart will land. "This isn't an exploding bullet, so you have to aim for something fleshy," he says.

"Will it go through clothes?"

"Any civilian body armor," Sam says.

"Do Vigilantes have body armor?" I ask. I line the sights up with the taxi sign on the car outside the window. I'm glad the passengers can't see into our car, or they'd freak the heck out.

"Sutherland will," Jax says. "And the committee. With the other Vigilantes, it depends on whether they are fighters who would get slowed down by it. It doesn't help you if you're shot in the face or get a dart to the hand or neck."

Yuck. Gruesome. I take a deep breath. I can do this. I have to.

"So who am I aiming for?" I ask. "Am I supposed to kill Sutherland?"

"No!" comes a chorus from the car, everyone at once.

"Okay!" I say. "Just checking."

"You've got her all fired up," Colette says.

"I can get us to HQ," Sam says. "And I can make sure we're not spotted."

"But," Jax says.

"But," Sam continues, "I don't have any clue how to stop this thing. Sutherland's obviously had it in the works for a couple years."

"He's choosing to initiate it right now, though," Jax says. "Something about the conditions is in his favor."

"Honestly," Sam says, "I think he had to move up his timeline because you busted out of jail. The longer you were a problem, the less credibility he had."

"Plus the vendetta," I add. "Jax has got a killer case for revenge. He's probably nervous that Jax is going to take him out."

But when I look over at Jax, he doesn't seem eager for battle. Just resigned and resolute.

17

JAX

What am I missing?

Colette continues to drive us toward the committee headquarters. Sam wires more off-grid tech into the car. Even Mia seems ready, pointing her dart gun at the windows and practicing a steady aim.

But my mind whirs. Jovana was recruited almost two years ago. Had to be, since she was set up in that slave bunker by the time I met her. Sutherland, or someone close to him, had to have falsified her information on the network.

After we blew up the sex slave operation, I didn't think I'd see her again, but she showed up two days later, picked up by a Phase Three. She was blubbering about the "hero who had bought her."

I took her in.

She behaved so believably, broken by her training, no longer saucy and spirited. That was the personality they had forced on her, she said.

In jail, thinking this over, I knew they had reviewed recordings of our interactions and decided that she had taken the wrong tack with me. So they came up with a new approach. I had no illusions by then that she had ever cared about me, or that the relationship we forged from her alleged "recovery" was real.

I just wanted revenge.

I had no idea how big this was. Or what a small role Jovana was actually playing in the overarching plot.

But why now? What is going on at HQ that Sutherland needs to stage this sort of grand-scale takeover?

"All right," Sam says, interrupting my thoughts. "Here's the overall layout of the facility." He brings up a map on the screen. "The committee members all have assigned entrances. Nobody comes in the same way." He points at yellow boxes. "Sutherland's offices are here." He jabs at a green section.

"The so-called War Room is over in this area." It lights up red. "Six floors underground. Two entrances. Both will have scanners. None of us with kill orders are going to be eligible to pass through." Sam glances back at us.

"So you're relying on me to get in?" Mia asks.

"Not sure that even you can make it," Sam says. "But at least the security won't snuff you as soon as you hit the first scan."

"They have that sort of system?" Colette asks.

"Hell yeah," Sam says. "Darts on every entrance."

"We should carry antidotes with us," Colette says.

"Yes," Sam says. "Although they may have their own cocktail."

"Great," she mutters. "Two darts in a day."

Sam hands me one of his pass keys, the type I used on the Missouri silo and the civilian car. "These have been very useful," I tell him.

"It isn't going to work anywhere important,

but it will help you move around the building," he says. "Just don't expect it to stop any scanners or darts."

I nod. I tuck the clear strip into a pocket. "I've verified that the weapon sweeps don't catch it."

Sam nods. "Good."

Both he and Colette look up as the HQ building looms ahead. It's a nondescript office building for a financial services company. But only the lobby and a few fake offices continue the ruse. The upper floors are all administrative, development, and tech offices. Below is where all the real action is. Steel and concrete bunkers with the mother lode of security.

Nobody gets out of there if the system itself doesn't want it. It's nominally monitored by humans, but the heart of the algorithm is determined by risk assessment and the information network that runs the U.S. syndicate.

And this computer system isn't going to care for us one bit.

"So do we just park out front?" Colette asks.

"Blend in with civilian traffic," Sam says.

We drive along the street and turn a corner to continue circling the building. "There's a hotel," I tell Colette. "Park in their garage. When we get out of this, we can meet back up here or get back together in two days in our usual spot."

"What's the usual spot?" Mia asks.

"You'll be with me," I tell her. "I'll take you."

"Should I know what it is?" Her voice is laced with panic.

Sam turns around in his seat. "A doughnut shop in Portland, Oregon. Voodoo." He lifts his case, which bears a sticker that says "I got VD in Portland."

Colette shakes her head. "I'd complain, but I love my Dirty Snowballs."

"Dirty Snowballs," Sam says reverently.

"Can we go kick some ass now?" Mia asks.

I squeeze her hand. "Sam and Colette, you go in the entrance designated for Marie Augusta." Sam looks at me. "She's in a wheelchair, so that one has slightly reprogrammed security. Might be easier to circumvent."

"Where you are headed, boss?" Sam asks.

"I have a hunch that when Mia goes in, something's going to happen that will muddy the security network. Plus, I'm supposedly dead. I'm waltzing right in the front door with her."

Sam nods. "I'll tap into the computer first shot I get. No telling when that will be. What's the endgame?"

"The War Room," I say. "Let's shake up the committee. Stop this thing."

"Or die trying," Sam says.

"Nobody's dying today," I remind him.

Colette parks the car in a dark corner of the garage. She pats the steering wheel affectionately. "I'll be back for you," she tells it.

I open my door. "We'll separate here," I tell them.

Colette heads out of the car and opens her trunk. "Let's take all I've got." She passes a slender case of vials to Jax.

"Where's that bag?" I ask Mia.

She heads to the backseat of the car to fetch it.

When she returns, Colette dumps several vials in. "They're unbreakable, so don't worry," she tells Mia. She packs a second set in Sam's tech bag.

"So I have one antidote for each dart, plus three of the new darts that don't need them," Mia says.

"That's right," Colette says. She kisses both of Mia's cheeks. "Stay strong and be smart."

Mia nods, and I can see her eyes tearing up a little.

Sam shakes my hand. "Good luck."

Mia hides her dart gun in her jacket. I don't know if security will let her take it in. I don't know how security is going to react to her at all.

Colette and Sam head out the opposite side of the garage. Mia and I walk down the entrance ramp and out into the sunny afternoon. It's late in the day. By the time we get done with this job, it will be night. I try not to think ahead. I've never gone into a situation with less of a plan than I have now.

We take our time walking the block back to the entrance of the office building. It's not terribly tall, four floors, and nondescript gray brick and steel. Mia's grip on my hand tightens as we approach the glass entrance. "What if they shoot us immediately?"

"Nothing will happen, not out here," I assure her. But I keep an eye on the scanner above us. It's already reading our heat signatures with an invisible beam.

I open the door.

Whatever's going to happen to us will occur inside.

18

MIA

The inside of the lobby is like any other. I glance at Jax as we enter the room. Red sofas are clustered around a large planter filled with flowers and leafy trees. A round marble desk holds a typical-looking security guy in a blue uniform. He blearily watches a few small screens.

It doesn't look anything like a silo or Vigilante stronghold, which I guess is the point.

A long desk ahead is manned by three receptionists, all young women with sleek hair and headsets.

"What happens now?" I ask.

"Those are Phase Fours behind the desk," Jax says quietly. "They're letting the others know we've arrived."

"What about that uniformed guy?"

"Phase Ten fighter," Jax says.

Really? "He doesn't look it," I say.

"Isn't meant to. He'd give me a run for my money, though," Jax says. "He might yet."

The man looks over at us.

"Should we talk to someone?" I ask.

"Let's see how far we can get," Jax says. "Up here where they try to appear normal, we can make our way safely, at least for a little while."

He leads me over to a bank of elevators, then thinks better of it and moves toward a stairwell.

"What's wrong with elevators?" I whisper.

"They are all fitted with gas," Jax says. "Let's not get trapped in our first sixty seconds."

A scanner blinks as we approach the door. "I think I should go first," I say, remembering how the Missouri silo worked. I had free run. "If it picks you first, you might get a dart."

He grins, and I can tell he's pleased with the way I'm working things out.

The lever on the door turns beneath my hand, and we go through.

"The War Room is several floors down," Jax says. "I have no illusions that we'll get anywhere near it without being stopped."

"It's just a question of what will stop us," I say. "People or the security system itself."

He points up. "Darts, cameras, the works."

I peer at the ceiling. There are a number of ordinary-looking gadgets. A camera with its wide glass eye. A sprinkler head. I suppose you could hide all manner of tech in those.

We hurry down a flight. The next door is locked tight. "Open it with the pass key or go on?" I ask.

"Let's go down," Jax says. His eyes are everywhere, watching the walls, the ceiling, the corners of every turn.

We head down the next flight. Nothing about the environment changes. No alarms sound. No warning lights flash. No darts fly at us.

The next door is also locked.

"Isn't the War Room six floors down?" I whisper.

Jax nods.

I take his hand and he squeezes it tightly. I have no idea when we'll hit our first roadblock. Or what I'll do if they dart Jax. Or me.

As we go down the third flight, the walls start to change. A clear acrylic covering sheathes the plaster. Jax stops us. "They're going to ID us now, like when we walked into that first silo."

I recognize the walls. They will project our information.

"Is there any way to fake this?" I ask.

"Heat signatures don't lie," he says.

But I have an idea. I take the dart gun out of my jacket. "Are they watching?" I ask.

"If they weren't, they're about to be."

I point the gun at his face. "Then you come with me."

Jax's expression shows no change, but I can feel his shoulders relax. He gets it. He knows what I'm about to do.

I walk ahead, jerking on his arm, aiming the dart at him. I see the first scanner device. It's like the one in the silo. I step into its range.

On the wall appears my screen, just my name, nothing else, same as always.

The dart gun is slightly behind me. As we

walk forward, the scanner picks up on it. My screen goes red. "Special is armed" flashes below my name.

"I have a prisoner," I call out. "I think you want him."

We take another step forward. Now Jax is in range.

His screen lights up red. "Jax De Luca. Executed 10-16-2020 09:06 a.m."

"That's going to confuse it," I say. Which was my intention. A human could make the leap that the information is wrong, but I'm not sure what a computer algorithm will do.

Heavy bold words flash on the screen. "Data system contaminated. Life signs present." The line about the execution goes away.

"Keep going," Jax says. "It won't dart me if it's trying to decide if I am dead."

I move faster now. We've gone down three flights. The screens follow us on the acrylic wall as we descend.

Jax's data alters as we go down. "Born 1984," it adds, as if trying to puzzle him out. "Entered Phase One training 1996."

We hurry along the stairs, assuming that we

are safe until a human intervenes.

Four flights down.

A grid appears ahead. Jax grabs my hand. He jerks a cufflink from his sleeve and tosses it into the grid. It incinerates, like in the car.

"What now?" I ask.

"We go in," he says.

We hurry back up to the previous door. Jax presses the pass key to the surface. The screen is now scrolling through Jax's history, trying to find the moment where its data is corrupted. Phase Two. Phase Six. Vegas syndicate. Promotion. Silo director. Faster and faster it churns.

The door clicks open.

Jax pulls off the pass key and pushes through. We're in a small receptionist area. Two exits. A woman sits behind a desk. She stands up, startled. "A special," she says, glancing at the wall behind us.

I glance behind. My status hasn't changed.

"I have a prisoner," I say, sticking to my first plan.

"I'll get someone," she says and disappears through one of the doors.

"Phase Five and still gets rattled," Jax murmurs. "That's why she's behind a desk."

"I don't think we should wait," I say to Jax. His screen is now at Ridley Prison, going through his activities there. It's slowed down, as if it thinks this is where the data no longer matches.

It gets to his escape and the red "FUGITIVE" blinks like it did when I met him.

We hurry to the opposite door. I don't even need the pass key because this one clicks on its own.

Inside is what appears to be a data center, a dozen men and women manning the big glass screens with information splashing across their surface.

"Pass through," Jax says. "Keep your gun on me, as that makes the computer think I'm under your control."

The people in the room still as we walk by. On a far screen, I see Sam and Colette's images. I hurry toward it.

"They're detained," Jax says. "Drag on the door on the map below them and it will unlock it."

But the boy by the screen turns with a fierce expression.

"I can't let you do that," he says.

I don't think twice, but shoot a dart into his arm. "What was that you said?" I ask Jax.

The boy crumples to the floor as the others gasp. I hear murmurs.

"What do we do with her?"

"She's a special."

Jax clears the door on the map and shoves the body of the boy aside as he types a few commands on the screen. Colette and Sam's images blink out. "They won't be followed for a while," Jax says.

The screens throughout the room begin to change. Jax's image takes over them all. "Fugitive. Kill order. Execution failed. No body cremated."

It's figured it out.

A couple of Vigilantes move toward me like they're going to do something, but I point at everyone who approaches. "Snuff dart," I say, knowing I'm lying but also knowing that the boy at my feet looks close enough for it to count. Only we know that he'll wake up in two hours.

Nobody comes toward us.

"Back door," Jax says.

We hurry past the screens and out the opposite door.

We enter a small lobby with only an open elevator car. "Going to have to risk the elevator now," Jax says. "I don't think they'll gas us. They're not touching you. And as long as the computer thinks you have me, we'll be fine."

We step in. "Fuck, I hate elevators," he says.

The doors close. There are no buttons inside.

"How does it know where we want to go?" I ask.

"It takes us where it wants us to go." Jax's eyes dart around the corners.

Then he says, "Shit."

"What?" I ask.

"I was wrong. They're gassing us."

I'm about to sharply inhale with shock, but Jax kisses me. His mouth is hot and roving and doesn't let up. I can't breathe, wanting to cry, not sure why he's doing this, as we're not fooling the computers anymore. But maybe it's a good-bye kiss. He knows the gas, and we're done for, and he doesn't want to say it.

It goes on and on and my lungs feel like they will burst. I become aware that he's pulled out the pass key and placed it on the door. There's an explosive burst of light, and a funnel of smoke curls around us.

Still, he won't break this kiss. He's passing air into me, keeping me calm. I want to panic, but the kiss won't let me. I feel my vision wanting to go, stars on the edges. He reaches behind me and forces open the doors, straining.

I sense a different sort of air coming in. Jax's hands come around my waist and he lifts me, shoving me up onto the floor that is revealed halfway up through the door.

I want to close my eyes, to sleep, but he keeps pushing until I fall back.

My knees come high as he forces my feet up and out of the elevator. I'm lying on the ground, a cold marble. Above me is a chandelier, bright and crystal.

The doors start to close and this gets my panic to rise. My adrenaline bursts and I sit up, moving to stop the doors, trying to make them stay open.

But they shut tight. I bang on the panels, but nothing moves in there. The elevator is still closed. I jump to my feet, looking for buttons to open the door, but there aren't any.

I want to wail and scream and cry. "JAX!" I call out, pounding on the door.

"You don't need to worry about him anymore," a voice says.

I turn around.

It's Sutherland.

I still have the dart gun. I aim it at his face. "I'm not going to go for your body armor," I say, willing my voice not to shake.

Sutherland holds out his arms. "It is my pleasure to finally make your acquaintance," he says smoothly. "You've caused quite a stir, bringing your captor right to our door."

My mind buzzes. Are they falling for the ruse? What could they know? That Jax kidnapped me, obviously. Then ditched me.

But then they took him from our hotel room.

So no, they aren't falling for it.

I aim the laser square on his forehead. "I hope you have an antidote for this new dart," I say.

Sutherland's expression wavers for just a second.

"System. Scan the gun," he commands.

A green beam cuts across the weapon.

"Under development," a computer voice says. "Technology unrecognized."

His lips twitch. "You're getting mighty big for your britches, Ms. Morrow," he says.

"Get Jax OUT of that elevator," I hiss. "I'm going to count to three."

"System. Take her out," he commands.

We're alone in the room. Is he talking to the computer?

Nothing happens.

"System," he commands. "Take out the special."

"System requires override by the committee for this command," the voice says.

"Send in my guards," he says.

I can see this isn't going to go my way. As soon as real people are involved, it's like Jax said, they can reassess the situation.

So I do the only thing I can think of.

I shoot him.

19

Jax

I got Mia out.

The silent gas hasn't gone anywhere. I don't doubt this even though it is odorless and invisible. Mia got a puff of it before I shoved her out, and it definitely affected her.

I'm on my knees, trying not to breathe, slowing my heart rate on purpose to buy me time. The panels are on lockdown now. The only thing that allowed me to part them in the first place was the last jolt of energy in the pass key. It's dead now.

I know how these elevators are made. It's why

I never, ever get in one. No hatches. No trapdoors. Just solid steel. And jets.

My chest burns. There is no point in using my phone. No way to call anyone. These elevators are black holes. No communications can get through.

I can hear the murmur of voices. I think one of them is Mia. A human must have run the gas. The system should protect her, especially now that she's away from me.

I got Colette and Sam out of detainment. Hopefully they'll make it.

I don't think I'm going to win here today, but maybe they'll escape at least. If the Vigilante network goes down, it goes down. My parents are out of it. Sam and Colette are out of it. Mia can't get hurt by it.

I've done my job.

I have to take a breath. I know this. My lungs feel like they are going to explode.

It's a sleeping gas. The old-fashioned kind. Silent, deadly, but a peaceful way to go. Among deaths, it's not the worst.

I sit down in the corner. If I'm going to think last thoughts, they'll be of Mia at least. Who would have known that this random girl holed up in a decommissioned safe house would be the perfect fit for a workaholic risk-driven Vigilante?

I picture her from that first meeting, how she slept so innocently as I slid the ropes around her body, tightening them inch by careful inch. I was so angry, so sure she was the cause of Klaus's disappearance. I couldn't see what she was. What she would be.

My vision starts to blur.

I can picture Klaus and his screwed-up blond hair. We were once friends. The betrayal stings one last time.

It's like he's in front of me. I want to strike out at his image, rage filling me. I throw a punch and realize with a jolt that it has connected.

"I know how you feel about elevators," he says.

There's a rush of air being sucked out. I realize we're moving, silently, down. I risk a breath, and it's clear. Klaus stands over me, tucking his cuff more neatly inside his suit jacket.

"I'm not here to save you," he quips and gives me a hand to stand up. "But I do need you to be alive a little longer."

"Who ordered the gas?" If it wasn't automatic,

then I'll know Mia is still safe.

"Some Phase Four with an itchy finger. She's been dealt with."

So Mia will be fine. I take in another deep breath. Time to finish this.

The minute I have enough energy to throw a punch, I do. We wrestle, falling out of the elevator and into a steel-lined hall.

I slam my elbow into his face. I'm not full force, not after the gas, but it's enough. I pin him to the ground. I'm ready to kill a second person with my bare hands.

I encircle his throat.

"It's Mia," he gasps. "War Room. Go in. Jovana's got her."

I look up. There's a door with no markings. But we've gone down a long way. Easily six floors below. The hallway is silent and empty.

I let go of Klaus. He sucks in a breath and rolls closer to the door. A green line scans him. "Klaus approved for entry to the War Room," a voice says.

Then it scans me.

I plan to jump into the room as soon as it opens for Klaus, but when the scanner is done, it says, "De Luca approved for entry to the War Room."

My suspicions are pricked. Why is the system allowing me in?

The question is moot as the door slides open.

We enter a room with a long oval table. A hush falls over the people seated at it as we walk in. I don't recognize anyone there, as I've had no cause to meet them, but I know this is the committee. They are watching a presentation.

Then I see her.

Jovana.

She's wearing a red dress, tightly fitted. Her hair is perfectly coiffed, like she's ready to go on a movie set. She's been talking. Her arm is still upraised, pointing at a towering screen behind her.

When she sees me, she drops her hand. "Well, look who has arrived. Exhibit A in how Sutherland has failed to keep the U.S. syndicate in line. Let's welcome Mr. Jax De Luca back from the dead."

I feel all the eyes on me.

Jovana keeps talking. "When Sutherland approached me with this idea for a global network, I saw the brilliance behind it. I helped him from every stage, recruiting the operatives to identify the weaknesses in the network."

She walks closer to me. "But Mr. De Luca here is a prime example of Sutherland's failed leadership. Jax broke out of Ridley Prison even with Vigilante surveillance."

An image behind her shows footage of me clocking the guard outside the prison.

"He also walked right into a high-security silo in Missouri, despite his fugitive status, and then he escaped it."

Another image shows me emerging from the hatch.

Mia is noticeably missing from these photos. She's been digitally erased.

"And as the final blow to the security and information integrity of this network, we have a dead man walking."

A few seconds of my crashing fall during the supposed execution play onscreen.

She leans forward, both hands braced on the table. The committee is rapt, hanging on her every word. "This is why Sutherland needs to be removed from power immediately."

Klaus rocks back on his heels. He seems very pleased with how everything has gone.

And that's when it hits me. I was chosen on purpose. Someone they could count on to beat the Vigilantes at their own game. To show their flaws, their weaknesses.

This was never about Sutherland.

It was always Jovana.

20

MIA

For several long seconds, I can only stare at Sutherland's body. I know it's just a stunner. That he'll wake up in a couple hours feeling like he's been on a bender.

But the security system goes bananas. Alarms flash and lights go off.

The girl who was in the room at first returns and stares down at Sutherland.

"It's just a drug," I say quickly. "He's not dead. He's not in any danger, even."

"System. Scan for respiration," she says.

A beam comes down and crosses Sutherland's body. "Respiration not registering," the voice says. "Subject deceased."

I stand there, mouth open. "No! He's not!" But then I remember that the new stuff made Jax pass for dead. That's why the execution was so convincing.

Crap.

I turn back to the elevator and bang on the door. "Jax!" I cry out. "What can I do?" I try to pry open the doors, but they are sealed.

Then suddenly I sense a movement behind the doors. The car is traveling down. "Jax?" I call out. "Are you in there?"

I turn my back to the door. I have to get to him. Is he dead already? Or did the movement of the elevator mean he got out?

I remember how Sutherland used voice commands and I call out, "System! Open the elevator!"

Nothing happens for a second. I can still feel the movement of the car. It's returning.

Then it stops. The doors open.

I rush in, expecting to find Jax's body on the ground.

But the elevator is empty.

I stand there, dumbfounded.

I hear noise, lots of noise, behind me. I turn around.

Suddenly the room is full of people, men, women, all holding weapons, and not just darts. Real guns.

"Where is Jax?" I ask them.

No one answers. They look at one another a moment, as if determining who has seniority now that Sutherland is down.

"What do we do?" one of the women asks. "She's a special."

"Take her downstairs," another man says. He's decked out in what looks like all-black vinyl armor, padded and sort of creepy. He's just designated himself the leader, apparently. "The committee can remove her status so she can be dealt with."

"Does she get to keep that thing?" another asks, a younger man who doesn't seem too certain about me.

I raise the gun again. "I'd like to see you take it," I say.

The vinyl-armor guy suddenly moves into action, a whirl of body parts, arms and legs. I don't even see the gun leave my hands, but suddenly he has it.

Whoa.

I step toward him. "Give me that back."

The guards look at each other. "Take her down," vinyl guy says. He turns the gun over to look at it. "This has to come from development. Figure out who let it get into the wrong hands." He tosses it to a woman in a normal blue dress.

His hand closes around my arm. "Let's go."

"I want my gun back," I say. "I'm a special. You can't ignore this."

Vinyl guy stops. "I can and I will."

"Can you?" I ask defiantly. "I'm not sure you are authorized."

"Nothing happening right now is addressed in the code," he says. His voice is gravelly and low. He's like Jax, only younger, and maybe bigger. It's hard to tell in all that gear.

But I'm going to show him. I haven't gotten as far as I have just to give up now.

"System," I call out. "I need protection."

A red grid flashes into place around me. The black-vinyl guy jerks back. He lifts his wrist to his mouth. "Someone manually override the system. We have a rogue special. I repeat, a rogue special."

I step backwards to the elevator. The grid follows me until I step inside the car. Then it blinks out.

"System. To the War Room," I say.

Sutherland is still on the floor, a medic in white kneeling next to him. Black-armor guy sneers at me. "Your time is limited," he says.

The doors close.

I sag against the wall. God. I shot Sutherland. And some random boy. My chest starts to heave, like I might hyperventilate. I try to calm it down. Am I cut out for this? Suddenly I'm not sure.

But I have to find Jax. And Sam and Colette are somewhere.

When the doors open, it's to a hallway that looks like it is lined with steel. The corridor is empty. Everything is deathly quiet.

There's a door ahead. I assume this is the War Room. As I approach it, a green beam rolls down my body and the bulk of the bag.

"No weapons or technology are allowed in the War Room," an electronic voice says.

I lower my arm and bring the bag with the antidotes around. "Can I take these?"

"Antidotes are unnecessary."

"But can I take them?"

"We can store them safely."

I'm arguing with a computer. A small, low door opens, reminding me of that first day in the silo, and a silver ball rolls out. The top opens with a hiss.

"Place the bag in the container. It will be returned only to Mia Morrow."

I set the bag inside. "Fine," I say.

The ball seals itself and rolls back into the wall.

"Morrow is approved for entry."

I turn back to the door. Time to face whatever's next.

21

JAX

The door opens and Mia stands there, looking apprehensive and alone.

She made it down. I knew she would.

Jovana spots her. "And look, now we have our rogue special, who has been running amok in the headquarters."

A screen changes above her head. It shows footage of Mia shooting Sutherland with the dart gun. He goes down instantly.

"Well, look at that," Jovana says. "It seems she just shot our Head of Syndicate."

Mia steps forward. "It was just a drug. It will wear off."

Jovana shakes her head. "Doesn't look like it to me."

The screen flashes "Subject deceased."

Mia seems to find her stride then and walks slowly and purposefully toward Jovana. "It's the same poison that fooled everyone with Jax." She waves at me. "And he's still standing."

The room visibly relaxes.

An elderly lady at the end of the table taps her cane against the edge. "This is no meeting for a special," she says. "She's untrained and a distraction from the work we must discuss here."

"Thank you," Jovana says.

"Aren't you a special?" Mia shoots back.

"I'm a trained Vigilante who was given special dispensation," Jovana says smoothly. She makes eye contact with the room, as any commanding speaker should.

I have to hand it to her. She's got this committee listening.

Jovana's voice is practically a purr now. "This puts me in the perfect position to carry out Sutherland's vision with competence and skill.

Unlike this messy business he's gotten us into."

I scan the room. Sam's intel was wrong, or else the second exit he mentioned is invisible. The War Room is lined with perfect steel, no seams, no lines, as if it was formed right here. The only break is the door. The roof curves upward in a dome shape, the banks of screens angling down.

As far as I can tell, no one can get in or out except through that single door.

Not that I'm interested in leaving. This has been a highly engrossing half hour.

Mia comes close to me and tugs at my hand. Several committee members take note of the gesture. I don't let go, even though she is telegraphing our allegiance.

Another committee member, a strong-jawed man in his late fifties, speaks up next. "What should we do with the special and Mr. De Luca?"

Jovana leans into the table again. "We should continue this hard line against Vigilante murder," she says. "We'll execute him properly, as should have been done to begin with, and then we'll clean up this mess we have overseas."

The room quiets.

"Who was next in line for Sutherland's

command?" the elderly woman asks.

Jovana smacks the table. "It doesn't matter! This is a new order for the Vigilante code. The old ways have not grown and expanded to manage the new information superstorage we have at our command. We need a global network, and we are perfectly suited to manage it from here."

The committee members start rumbling among themselves.

"What should we do?" Mia whispers in my ear.

"Just hang tight," I say. None of this has played out the way I expected.

"But they said they would execute you," Mia protests.

"I'll be fine," I say.

Another elderly lady stands up with slow, easy grace. "Ms. Lukova, while we appreciate the vision you have presented to us, I see no reason to go off on this venture half-cocked. We've had significant strife in the past twenty-four hours. I propose we delay this meeting until we can sort through the chaos."

The other members of the committee murmur in agreement, other than the cane lady at the end of the table, who scowls.

The gentleman who spoke earlier says, "I say we bring this to a voice-authenticated vote. Every action of this committee regarding structure and leadership must be unanimous."

More murmurs.

"System," the man says. "Prepare the vote."

The screens above show seven photographs matching the committee members at the table. Next to them are large green and red boxes with "Yes" and "No" inside.

"Nay," says the man. A digital audiowave checks his voice, then a check mark appears next to "No."

The poised older woman is next. "Nay."

Her voice is authenticated as well.

"That's enough," Jovana snaps.

She steps back from the table. I recognize the smirk on her face and immediately my senses go on alert. She's about to do something unexpected.

She coughs into her hand as if she's swallowed something. "Water, please," she chokes out, waving to a pitcher at the end of the table.

The elderly man picks up the pitcher, plucking it from a circle of glasses.

My neck hair prickles. Why is she asking for this now? The timing is off.

I pull Mia to me. Something's wrong with the water, the way it pours. It's too slow. The man sees it too, he's trained, but he's too late. The first splash hits the bottom of the glass and the room fills with the sound of an explosion.

I drag Mia to the floor. The boom is deafening. Smoke fills the air.

"Lockdown!" I hear Jovana cry.

The system responds, and the lights over the door go out.

The screens all change as scanners go through the room, seeking out damage. Next to each committee member is a health report. The sound of coughing and choking drowns out everything.

The explosion was small, but the smoke and chemical gas are debilitating. I pull a handkerchief out of my pocket and press it to Mia's mouth.

One of the committee members tries to open the door, but it's sealed shut.

"System," one shouts. "Open the door."

The screens flash. "Lockdown activated. Unanimous authentication required."

"What's that?" Mia asks.

I can barely make her out in the smoke. "During lockdown, the system requires everyone to agree to open the doors. Safety precaution."

The scanners continue to assess damage, listing concerns.

Respiration labored.

Third-degree burns.

Something catches my eye and I see Jovana climbing a synthetic rope toward a hatch in the ceiling.

The other exit.

I stand up to go after her, but Klaus spots me and slams a fist into my face. I push Mia out of the way as I turn to fight him.

"I'm not drugged this time, Klaus," I say to him.

He delivers a roundhouse kick to my legs, but I easily turn aside and grab his knee, twisting him down onto the floor.

I look up. Jovana's at the hatch.

But Mia is right behind her.

The screens flash, waiting for authentication. "Open," a feeble voice calls out.

A check mark appears by the image of one woman.

The others start to find their voices. "Open," cries another. Then another.

The check marks appear as the scanners finish their round.

The last image is the man who poured the water. An arrow pulses by his name. Then it switches to "Deceased."

Klaus jumps up and lands a punch while I'm wondering how we'll unlock the door if we require a unanimous vote from a dead man.

I bend over, accepting the blow, and decide I've had enough of him. I spin into an elbow to his gut, then a hard uppercut to his jaw, enough to cause a concussion. He goes down hard. Klaus never was a fighter.

I look up. Mia has tied several knots around Jovana's ankles, stopping her. Jovana is trying to undo them, awkwardly, hanging from the rope, but the knots are good.

That's my girl.

"We can't get out," a woman next to me says. "Duran is dead."

The screen flashes another warning. "Air contamination reaching critical levels."

One of the men near me collapses on the table.

"System," someone calls. "Move Duran to next in command."

Duran's image slides to another screen, still pulsing a red "Deceased."

The scanners register the other occupants of the room. Klaus. Jovana. Me. Mia.

Klaus's image moves to another screen with the words "Reported deceased. Situation unknown."

Then so does mine, alongside the words "Reported executed. Situation unknown."

Jovana laughs from above. "I'm next in command. I'm not letting you out. When you are all dead, I'll be in charge anyway." She kicks at the knots.

But the screen drops in the picture of Mia.

"Next in command, Mia Morrow."

"Open the door," Mia calls out.

A check box appears. Behind us, the sealed door hisses on its pneumatic seal.

Immediately a medic trolley rolls in, followed by a dozen armed guards.

It's chaos in the smoke and crowd as committee members are helped out of the room.

Blowers begin sucking the air from the room, out the door. At the top hatch, Jovana still struggles with the knots on her legs.

Mia lands on the center of the table and jumps toward me.

I catch her.

"You're on the committee," I say to her.

"Does that mean I get to boss you around?" she says.

I drag her in close to me. "I am at your mercy."

I hold her tight, watching the guards evacuate the men and women. The air is already almost clear.

"Cut that one down," I say, pointing up at the hatch.

The guard standing near looks up. "Cut who?"

Mia and I look up.

Jovana is gone.

22

MIA

In the hall outside the War Room, I don't want to let go of Jax's hand. I'm still shaking from what happened. My throat is raw from the chemical smoke.

Several of the committee members have been laid out on stretchers and are being wheeled to the elevator.

"How do we find Colette and Sam?" I ask Jax.

"They'll find their way out. When a committee member dies, all kill orders and jurisdiction changes are put on hold." He strokes my hair. "We may be getting doughnuts after all."

The one poised lady leans against the wall close by. A medic gives her a mask for oxygen, and she breathes from it steadily, watching me with kind, sharp eyes beneath a curly mass of white hair.

She gestures for me to come near.

I release Jax and go over to her. "You okay?" I ask.

She hands the oxygen mask back to the medic. "Mia Morrow," she says. "I know who you are."

"You do?" I ask. "Nobody seems to know me at all!"

She smiles, pushing a curl back from her forehead. She has a cut on the back of her hand, and the medic reaches for it. She waves him away. "I'm fine," she says.

She threads her arm through mine. "I had hoped to meet you one day. I knew your great-grandfather, Prescott. He was about to retire, and I was just a young Phase Two. Your mother was about three years old. She was a cute little thing, tearing through the silos. I think she was the reason he left the service."

My voice is barely audible. "You — you met my mother?"

"She was just a toddler then. I didn't know her as a young woman. I was in an entirely different syndicate."

My heart hammers. This is someone who knows who I am! "Was my mother a Vigilante, then?"

"She was."

"My parents died in a boating accident."

Her eyes flash with remorse. "I'm not aware of the circumstances of their death. I just know that I signed the papers naming you a special. And that you were to be protected at all cost. It required a rather unusual arrangement, but no one wanted Prescott's last surviving family member to be lost to us."

"Who was my Aunt Bea?"

"Georgiana Powers was a faithful, long-serving Vigilante. When her husband was killed in action, she holed herself up in that safe house. We gave you to her in hopes that you would give her some purpose again. I'd say we succeeded in that."

My stomach turns. "She wasn't my aunt, then?"

The woman shakes her head. "Your mother was an only child. Vigilantes do not often have many children. It's a hard life."

My knees feel weak. I hold a hand out to steady myself against the wall, but Jax is there, hanging on to me. I sink against him.

The woman squeezes my arm. "We'll take care of the matter of the committee. This was just a temporary assignment. We have members-in-waiting who will take the place of Duran. He was a fine man." She shakes her head. "Such a pity Sutherland put any trust in that horrid woman."

"You ready, Ms. Young?" a medic asks. "We'll take you topside now."

She nods.

"Wait," I call out.

She turns back to me.

"Can I be a Vigilante, then?" I ask.

She smiles. "Of course. You are all that is left of the original line. You only need to ask."

The medic leads her away.

Jax's strong arms come around me. He kisses the top of my head. "So is that what you plan to do?" he asks. "Start your Phase One training?"

I turn around in his embrace and look up at him. Beautiful, sleek, perfectly dressed Jax. You'd never tell from the look of him that he'd been executed that morning, run miles in pajama pants, nearly suffocated in an elevator, and survived a chemical explosion. I could never make Vigilantism look as good as he did.

"Can I just get the shoes?" I ask. "Somebody blew up my first pair."

His megawatt smile is like a room lighting up. "Perhaps, if it's the only thing you wear."

And he kisses me, the currents of air still blowing around us, the medics carting people to the elevator, and guards clearing out the War Room.

I will go wherever he does. Vigilante. Civilian. Dart guns or ropes.

I'm his.

Epilogue

MIA

Six Months Later

Jax looks so much like a sheep herder from a Swiss children's book that I have to laugh out loud.

He hurries down the side of the hill at a half run, half gallop. His hair blows wildly. He's wearing goofy green shorts and a white collared shirt. All he needs is a pair of suspenders to complete the ensemble.

Spring in the Alps is breathtaking and much easier to manage than the winter, not that I was here that much. After leaving the Vigilante headquarters in D.C., we agreed I would go through Phase One training in Missouri with Alan Carter while Jax helped establish some order in the syndicates ravaged by Sutherland and Jovana's plan to undercut their authority.

Sutherland was decommissioned, and Colette and Sam reinstated. Jovana went off grid again. Jax hasn't decided what to do about Klaus. Currently he is working a Vigilante desk job in some rural area.

I was a model Vigilante trainee, already well schooled in a number of basics, including knot tying, dart guns, and engaging the enemy.

I got my own pair of Phase One shoes. I ran into Katya, who was just about to graduate to Phase Two. I apologized for the way I stole her shoes. She shrugged and said she learned a valuable lesson about never letting anyone, no matter how innocent seeming, learn about her food allergies.

"At least you called the medic after doctoring the tea," she said. "A real enemy wouldn't."

I didn't know what sort of place Katya would find among the Vigilantes. I'd check up on her later, see where she ended up.

The wind picks up on the hillside, ruffling the

waves of colorful wildflower blooms. The chateau Jax bought me to replace my blown-up house is small and cozy and all mine. It's been paradise here, but a faint restlessness has started to build in me again since my Phase One training ended and we both left the network.

Jax makes it down to where I'm marking the spots where I have stubbornly planted watermelon seeds, despite warnings from the locals that they will never grow in this soil. I remember cutting fat green fruit from the vines with my parents, and I'm determined to bring some small part of my heritage with me, even as far away as I find myself now.

"Who was the man who came by?" I ask. Jax is returning from greeting a visitor, a rare event as remote as we are from any decent-sized cities.

"Just a delivery," he says and kisses the top of my head. "Any sprouts yet?"

I press down on the damp earth beneath my fingers. "Still hoping," I say.

"They'll come."

He sits down next to me. The sun is low on the horizon, turning the mountaintops in the distance a warm gold. I scoot up next to him on the soft grass at the edge of my little garden.

He fingers the bottom of my cotton shirt, finding a strip of skin.

"You know what I love most about living out here?" he asks.

I lean into him. "What?"

"Stripping you naked under a bright blue sky."

His eyes are mischievous as his hand slips beneath my soft shirt.

"Is that your plan right now?" I ask.

"Maybe."

With lightning reflexes, he whips the shirt over my head and nuzzles into my neck. "You make me crazy running around without a bra." He leans down and captures a tightened nipple with his teeth.

I fall back into the undulating grass. His dark head roves over my body, nipping with little kisses. One thing is for certain, no matter how long we're together, this part never gets old.

The sun is just a glimmer of red by the time we slip back into our clothes.

I roll onto my back, and something presses into my spine, small and hard. I sit up. It's a small box wrapped in parchment.

"Was this your delivery?" I ask, holding it up.

The last vestiges of sunset burnish his skin in

194

red gold. "It's for you."

My heart speeds up a little. It's awfully small. Ring-box size. Maybe it's some other piece of jewelry.

I tear away the brown paper, revealing a black velvet box.

I take a deep breath.

Jax covers my hand with his before I open it. "Just know that I'm behind you, whatever you decide to do. Vigilante or not. Service or home. Stateside or here." He turns the box on my palm and lifts the lid.

It's a ring.

The diamond is square and so big it seems to fill the space. I look up from it, at his pleased, happy face.

"I'll go wherever you go," he says, "as long as you'll say you'll marry me."

My gaze slides back down to the ring. I want this. I know I do. I love him. I know that too. But the restlessness still vibrates within me. How do I know Jax means it? How does he know himself?

His Blackphone buzzes in his pocket. He ignores it, but it keeps going, breaking the spell.

"Check it," I say.

He nods and pulls it out. "It's Sam," he says. He hits the button for speakerphone.

"Hello, Sam," I say. "How are things in D.C.?"

"Crazy shitpots," he says. "You had enough mountains and lakes yet? I got the perfect job for a new Phase Two."

I look back down at the ring. I know we're going to get to that place eventually. I know I want it. But I also want to know for sure that we've figured out the rest of it. Our careers. Our lives.

"Sam, we're getting on a plane," I say. "See you stateside sometime tomorrow."

"Excellent," he says. "Only bring that deadbeat boyfriend of yours if you can't figure out anywhere to stash his body."

Jax lifts his eyebrows. "She knows exactly where to stash me."

"Aw, man! Now I have to scrub my ears with soap," Sam laughs. "Over and out, kids." The call disconnects.

Jax takes the box from me. "Is this a no, then?" His voice has an edge to it, like he's masking his feelings.

"I want to marry you," I assure him. But I

close the box in his hand. "Can you ask me again after my first real Vigilante mission?"

He holds my gaze in his, then leans in to settle a soft, warm kiss on my mouth. "Of course I can. I'll wait all my life."

The sun disappears behind the mountains as we stand up and head back to the chateau. I take a look around at the shadows forming on the hillside as we approach full dark. I won't be here to see if my watermelon seeds manage to sprout.

But I'm doing the right thing.

I take Jax's hand and pull him along with me. He dragged me into this world of Vigilantes, danger, risk, and intrigue. He tied me up and stripped me down and thrust me right into the middle of it all.

So I'm going to drag him right back.

You've reached the end
of the Vigilante's Lover series!

We might write another book in the Vigilante world. I know I'm excited to see Mia's first mission.

Join the mail list to make sure
you don't miss a release!

www.anniewinters.com

If you love Annie's writing style, check out her books under her pen names:

USA Today bestselling **JJ Knight** for suspense serials grounded in the real world (no spies!)

USA Today bestselling **Deanna Roy** for standalone emotional romances without cliffhangers.